Sharper Than a Serpent's Tooth . . .

Brule swept aside some tapestries in a dim corner nook and, drawing Kull with him, stepped behind them. Kull could hear the breeze in the other room blowing the window curtains about, and it seemed to him like the murmur of ghosts. Then through the door, stealthily, came Tu, chief councilor of the king.

He came with upraised dagger, walking silently. A moment he halted, gazing about the apparently empty room, which was lighted dimly by a single candle. Then he advanced cautiously, apparently at a loss to understand the absence of the king.

Kull with a single mighty leap hurled himself into the room. Tu spun, but the blinding, tigerish speed of the attack gave him no chance for defense or counterattack. Sword steel flashed in the dim light and grated on bone as Tu toppled backward, Kull's sword standing out between his shoulders.

Kull leaned above him, teeth bared in the killer's snarl, heavy brows a-scowl above eyes that were like the gray ice of the cold sea. Then he released the hilt and recoiled, shaken, dizzy, the hand of death at his spine.

For as he watched, Tu's face became strangely dim and unreal; the features mingled and merged in a seemingly impossible manner. Then, like a fading mask of fog, the face suddenly vanished and in its stead gaped and leered a *monstrous serpent's head!*

"Valka!" gasped Kull, sweat beading his forehead, and again: "Valka!"

Brule leaned forward, face immobile. Yet his glittering eyes mirrored something of Kull's horror.

"Regain your sword, lord king," said he. "There are yet deeds to be done."

THE ROBERT E. HOWARD LIBRARY

Cormac Mac Art
Kull

Forthcoming:
Solomon Kane
Bran Mak Morn
Eons of the Night
Trails in Darkness
Beyond the Borders

KULL

ROBERT E. HOWARD

KULL

Baen Publishing Enterprises
P.O. Box 1403
Riverdale, N.Y. 10471

ISBN: 0-671-87673-2

Cover art by C.W. Kelly

First printing, July 1995

Distributed by
SIMON & SCHUSTER
1230 Avenue of the Americas
New York, N.Y. 10020

Printed in the United States of America

CONTENTS

INTRODUCTION:

THE HUMAN SIDE

Kull was Robert E. Howard's first attempt at writing stories in a past created from the whole cloth—a world in which kingdoms like those of accepted history exist "before the dawn of time," alongside monstrous survivors of a still dimmer past. This is the fantasy sub-genre in which Howard later placed the Conan stories, his own most successful series and a series more successful than the many, many attempts of others to follow the trail Howard blazed.

Kull wasn't a commercially successful character for Howard during his lifetime, though. Farnsworth Wright, the editor of *Weird Tales* during its great period during the late '20s and '30s, was the primary market for most of Howard's fantasy. Wright bought only "The Shadow Kingdom" and "The Mirrors of Tuzun Thune" of the Kull tales. After Howard's death Wright also took the poem "The King and the Oak." The remaining Kull stories, with two partial exceptions, didn't see print until republication of the Conan stories in the 1960s inspired a sword & sorcery boom.

I said "two partial exceptions." Kull is a supporting character in "Kings of the Night," a later-written story about a Pictish chieftain living ca 200 AD, in the historical past rather than in Howard's invented Pre-Cataclysmic Age. I like "Kings of the Night" a great deal and I hope you'll read it in the forthcoming collection *Bran Mak Morn*, but Kull isn't the main focus. Mind, if there'd been more Bran stories and fewer about Kull, I'd have moved "Kings" here in an eyeblink.

The other exception is " 'By This Axe I Rule!' " Some years after Howard failed to sell it in the original form, he rewrote the piece as the first Conan story, " The Phoenix on the Sword." Wright bought that version, and it's widely regarded as one of Howard's best works.

Presumably all ten completed Kull stories were offered to *Weird Tales*. As a general rule, when Wright rejected a story by Robert E. Howard, the story wasn't terribly good. Two of the rejected Kull stories (" 'By This Axe I Rule!' " and "Delcardes' Cat") are, in my opinion, very good indeed, and the others are at least up to the normal level of *Weird Tales* fiction. Why were they rejected?

The Kull stories weren't likely to have offended Wright's sense of sexual propriety the way "The Frost-Giant's Daughter" almost certainly did (Conan sees a beautiful girl on the icy waste; he pursues, intending to rape her). In fact, Howard notes a number of times that Kull isn't particularly interested in women.

There's a dreamy, poetic quality to the Kull stories that's unusual for Howard's work. This may not have been Wright's view of where Howard's commercial value lay. On the other hand, the quality's just as marked in a story which Wright bought, "The Mirrors of Tuzun Thune," as it is in "Delcardes' Cat" and "The Striking of the Gong" which he rejected.

A lot of editorial decisions come down to whim. Maybe that was the case here; particularly since, in the late '20s when the Kull stories were probably written, Howard wasn't the huge name that he became after the success of Conan.

With " 'By This Axe I Rule!' " and "The Phoenix on the Sword" we're on firmer ground. The differences between the two versions are probably the reasons, in Wright's mind, to reject the first and buy the second. Since "The Phoenix on the Sword" was the first-published Conan story, it wasn't simply a matter of the character himself being more popular.

" 'By This Axe I Rule!' " isn't as well written as the Conan version. Howard had improved his technique by practice during the three or four years between writing the two stories. There's nothing obviously wrong about the line by line quality of the Kull story, though. Wright published far worse prose, some of it by Howard, so I don't believe that was the problem.

A much more significant difference is that "The Phoenix on the Sword" has major, overt fantasy elements: an evil wizard, a magic ring, a demon baboon, and a saint dead 1500 years acting as the story's *deus ex machina*. The only fantasy in " 'By This Axe I Rule!' " is that it's set in a "time" that is itself fantastic, a non-existent world.

There's a final distinction between the two stories that, for me, makes " 'By This Axe I Rule!' " one of Howard's most powerful stories. Kull's real struggle isn't against the band of assassins bursting into his bedchamber. Rather, he's being smothered by the traditions of the empire which he rules in name but which was old before Kull's ancestral islands rose from the sea. The climax of the Conan story is in slaughter which copies Kull's battle stroke for stroke. " 'By This Axe I Rule!' " climaxes only afterwards, as Kull stands in the bloody shambles to shatter the chains of custom which until then have shackled his kingship and his humanity.

That same focus on Kull as a man infuses most of the stories of the series. Some of the pieces are minor, but they're all a good read for their length. More than Conan, I think Kull was Howard's fictional self-portrait: an intelligent man from beyond the fringes of real civilization, trying to understand a world in which he'd had more success than most of the better-educated, more urbane people who were now his fellows.

Besides the completed stories, this collection includes three fragments. I've read a lot of Howard fragments and in another series have finished one of them for publication. The longest of these three is the only fragment I've read that made me really wish that Howard had completed it himself.

The Kull fragments are here presented as the author left them. There's enough of Howard's prose to fill this volume without me intruding on his thoughts, his conceptions. I could add nothing that I consider of real importance to these fragments by finishing them. If you want more complete stories with the texture only Robert E. Howard could give them, well, watch for the next volumes of this series.

—Dave Drake

PROLOG

Of that epoch known by the Nemedian chroniclers as the Pre-Cataclysmic Age, little is known except the latter part, and that is veiled in the mists of legendry. Known history begins with the waning of the Pre-Cataclysmic civilization, dominated by the kingdoms of Kamelia, Valusia, Verulia, Grondar, Thule, and Commoria. These peoples spoke a similar language, arguing a common origin. There were other kingdoms, equally civilized, but inhabited by different, and apparently older, races.

The barbarians of that age were the Picts, who lived on islands far out on the western ocean; the Atlanteans, who dwelt on a small continent between Pictish Islands and the main, or Thurian, continent; and the Lemurians, who inhabited a chain of large islands in the eastern hemisphere.

There were vast regions of unexplored land. The civilized kingdoms, though enormous in extent, occupied a comparatively small portion of the whole planet. Valusia was the westernmost kingdom of the Thurian Continent; Grondar the easternmost. East of Grondar, whose people were less highly cultured than those of the other kingdoms, stretched a wild and barren expanse of deserts. Among the less arid stretches, in the jungles, and among the mountains, lived scattered clans and tribes of primitive savages. Far to the South there was a mysterious civilization, unconnected with the Thurian culture, and apparently pre-human in its nature. On the far eastern shores of the continent there lived another race, human, but mysterious and non-Thurian, with whom the Lemurians from time to time came in contact. They apparently came from a shadowy and nameless continent lying somewhere east of the Lemurian Islands.

The Thurian civilization was crumbling; their armies were composed largely of barbarian mercenaries. Picts, Atlanteans, and Lemurians were their generals, their statesmen, often their kings. Of the bickerings of the kingdoms, and the wars between Valusia and Commoria, as well as the conquests by which the Atlanteans founded a kingdom on the mainland, there are more legends than accurate history.

—The Hyborian Age

EXILE OF ATLANTIS

The sun was setting. A last crimson glory filled the land and lay like a crown of blood on the snow-sprinkled peaks. The three men who watched the death of the day breathed deep the fragrance of the early wind which stole up out of the distant forests, and then turned to a more material task. One of the men was cooking venison over a small fire, and this man, touching a finger to the smoking viand, tasted with the air of a connoisseur.

"All ready, Kull—Khor-nah; let us eat."

The speaker was young—little more than a boy: a tall, slim-waisted, broad-shouldered lad who moved with the easy grace of a leopard. Of his companions, one was an older man, a powerful, massively-built, hairy man with an aggressive face. The other was a counterpart of the speaker, except for the fact that he was slightly larger—taller, a thought deeper of chest and broader of shoulder. He gave the impression, even more than the first youth, of dynamic speed concealed in long, smooth muscles.

"Good," said he, "I am hungry."

"When were you ever otherwise, Kull?" jeered the first speaker.

"When I am fighting," Kull answered seriously.

The other shot a quick glance at his friend so as to fathom his inmost mind; he was not always sure of his friend.

7

"And then you are blood-hungry," broke in the older man. "Am-ra, have done with your bantering and cut us food."

Night began to fall; the stars blinked out. Over the shadowy hill country swept the dusk wind. Far off, a tiger roared suddenly. Khor-nah made an instinctive motion toward the flint-pointed spear which lay beside him. Kull turned his head, and a strange light flickered in his cold gray eyes.

"The striped brothers hunt tonight," said he.

"They worship the rising moon." Am-ra indicated the east where a red radiance was becoming evident.

"Why?" asked Kull. "The moon discloses them to their prey and their enemies."

"Once, many hundreds of years ago," said Khor-nah, "a king tiger, pursued by hunters, called on the woman in the moon, and she flung him down a vine whereby he climbed to safety and abode for many years in the moon. Since then, all the striped people worship the moon."

"I don't believe it," said Kull bluntly. "Why should the striped people worship the moon for aiding one of their race who died so long ago? Many a tiger has scrambled up Death Cliff and escaped the hunters, but they do not worship that cliff. How should they know what took place so long ago?"

Khor-nah's brow clouded. "It little becomes you, Kull, to jeer at your elders or to mock the legends of your adopted people. This tale must be true, because it has been handed down from generation unto generation longer than men remember. What always was, must always be."

"I don't believe it," reiterated Kull. "These mountains always were, but someday they will crumble and vanish. Someday the sea will flow over these hills—"

"Enough of this blasphemy!" cried Khor-nah with a passion that was almost anger. "Kull, we are close friends, and I bear with you because of your youth; but one thing you must learn: respect for tradition. You mock at the customs and ways of our people; you whom that people rescued from the wilderness and gave a home and a tribe."

"I was a hairless ape roaming in the woods," admitted Kull frankly and without shame. "I could not speak the language of men, and my only friends were the tigers and the wolves. I know not whom my people were, or what blood am I—"

"That matters not," broke in Khor-nah. "For all you have the aspect of one of that outlaw tribe who lived in Tiger Valley, and who perished in the Great Flood, it matters little. You have proven yourself a valiant warrior and a mighty hunter—"

"Where will you find a youth to equal him in throwing the spear or in wrestling?" broke in Am-ra, his eyes alight.

"Very true," said Khor-nah. "He is a credit to the Sea-mountain tribe, but for all that, he must control his tongue and learn to reverence the holy things of the past and of the present."

"I mock not," said Kull without malice. "But many things the priests say I know to be lies, for I have run with the tigers and I know wild beasts better than the priests. Animals are neither gods nor fiends, but men in their way without the lust and greed of the man—"

"More blasphemy!" cried Khor-nah angrily. "Man is Valka's mightiest creation."

Am-ra broke in to change the subject. "I heard the coast drums beating early in the morning. There is war on the sea. Valusia fights the Lemurian pirates."

"Evil luck to both," grunted Khor-nah.

Kull's eyes flickered again. "Valusia! Land of Enchantment! Someday I will see the great City of Wonder."

"Evil the day that you do," snarled Khor-nah. "You will be loaded with chains, with the doom of torture and death hanging over you. No man of our race sees the Great City save as a slave."

"Evil luck attend her," muttered Am-ra.

"Black luck and a red doom!" exclaimed Khor-nah, shaking his fist toward the east. "For each drop of spilt Atlantean blood, for each slave toiling in their cursed galleys, may a black blight rest on Valusia and all the Seven Empires!"

Am-ra, fired, leaped lithely to his feet and repeated part of the curse; Kull cut himself another slice of cooked meat.

"I have fought the Valusians," said he. "And they were bravely arrayed but not hard to kill. Nor were they evil featured."

"You fought the feeble guard of her northern coast," grunted Khor-nah. "Or the crew of stranded merchant ships. Wait until you have faced the charge of the Black Squadrons, or the Great Army, as have I. *Hai!* Then there is blood to drink! With Gandaro of the Spear, I harried the Valusian coasts when I was younger than you, Kull. Aye, we carried the torch and the sword deep into the empire. Five hundred men we were, of all the coast tribes of Atlantis. Four of us returned! Outside the village of Hawks, which we burned and sacked, the van of the Black Squadrons smote us. *Hai*, there the spears drank and the swords were eased of thirst! We slew and they slew, but when the thunder of battle was stilled, four of us escaped from the field, and all of us sore wounded."

"Ascalante tells me," pursued Kull, "that the walls about the Crystal City are ten times the height of a tall man; that the gleam of gold and silver would dazzle the eyes, and the women who throng the streets or lean from their windows are robed in strange, smooth robes that rustle and sheen."

"Ascalante should know," grimly said Khor-nah, "since he was slave among them so long that he forgot his good Atlantean name and must forsooth abide by the Valusian name they gave him."

"He escaped," commented Am-ra.

"Aye, but for every slave that escapes the clutches of

the Seven Empires, seven are rotting in dungeons and dying each day, for it was not meant for an Atlantean to bide as a slave."

"We have been enemies to the Seven Empires since the dawn of time," mused Am-ra.

"And will be until the world crashes," said Khor-nah with a savage satisfaction. "For Atlantis, thank Valka, is the foe of all men."

Am-ra rose, taking his spear, and prepared to stand watch. The other two lay down on the sward and dropped off to sleep. Of what did Khor-nah dream? Battle perhaps, or the thunder of buffalo, or a girl of the caves. Kull—

Through the mists of his sleep echoed faintly and far away the golden melody of the trumpets. Clouds of radiant glory floated over him; then a mighty vista opened before his dream self. A great concourse of people stretched away into the distance, and a thunderous roar in a strange language went up from them. There was a minor note of steel clashing, and great shadowy armies reined to the right and the left; the mist faded and a face stood out boldly, a face above which hovered a regal crown—a hawk-like face, dispassionate, immobile, with eyes like the gray of the cold sea. Now the people thundered again: "Hail the king! Hail the king! *Kull the king!*"

Kull awoke with a start—the moon glimmered on the distant mountains, the wind sighed through the tall grass. Khor-nah slept beside him and Am-ra stood, a naked bronze statue against the stars. Kull's eyes wandered to his scanty garment: a leopard's hide twisted about his pantherish loins. A naked barbarian—Kull's cold eyes glimmered. Kull the king! Again he slept.

They arose in the morning and set out for the caves of the tribe. The sun was not yet high when the broad blue river met their gaze and the caverns of the tribe rose to view.

"Look!" Am-ra cried out sharply. "They burn someone!"

A heavy stake stood before the caves; thereon was a young girl bound. The people who stood about, hard-eyed, showed no sign of pity.

"Sareeta," said Khor-nah, his face setting into unbending lines. "She married a Lemurian pirate, the wanton."

"Aye," broke in a stony-eyed old woman. "My own daughter; thus she brought shame on Atlantis. My daughter no longer! Her mate died; she was washed ashore when their ship was broken by the craft of Atlantis."

Kull eyed the girl compassionately. He could not understand—why did these people, her own kind and blood, frown on her so, merely because she chose an enemy of her race? In all the eyes that were centered on her, Kull saw only one trace of sympathy. Am-ra's strange blue eyes were sad and compassionate.

What Kull's own immobile face mirrored there is no knowing. But the eyes of the doomed girl rested on his. There was no fear in her eyes, but a deep and vibrant appeal. Kull's gaze wandered to the fagots at her feet. Soon the priest, who now chanted a curse beside her, would stoop and light these with the torch which he now held in his left hand. Kull saw that she was bound to the stake with a heavy wooden chain, a peculiar thing which was typically Atlantean in its manufacture. He could not sever that chain, even if he reached her through the throng that barred his way. Her eyes implored him. He glanced at the fagots, touched the long flint dagger at his girdle. She understood, nodded, relief flooding her eyes.

Kull struck as suddenly and unexpectedly as a cobra. He snatched the dagger from his girdle and threw it. Fairly under the heart it struck, killing her instantly. While the people stood spellbound, Kull wheeled, bounded away, and ran up the sheer side of the cliff for twenty feet, like a cat. The people stood, struck dumb; then a man whipped up bow and arrow and sighted along the smooth shaft. Kull was heaving himself over the lip of the cliff; the bowman's eyes narrowed—Am-ra, as if by accident, lurched headlong into him, and the arrow sang wide and aside. Then Kull was gone.

He heard the screaming on his track; his own tribesmen, fired with the blood-lust, wild to run him down and slay him for violating their strange and bloody code of morals. But no man in Atlantis could outrun Kull of the Sea-mountain tribe.

Kull eludes his infuriated tribesmen, only to fall captive to the Lemurians. For the next two years he toils as a slave at the oars of a galley, before escaping. He makes his way to Valusia, where he becomes an outlaw in the hills, until captured and confined in her dungeons. Fortune smiles upon him; he becomes, successively, a gladiator in the arena, a soldier in the army, and a commander. Then, with the backing of the mercenaries and certain discontented Valusian noblemen, he strikes for the throne. Kull it is who slays the despotic King Borna and rips the crown from his gory head. The dream has become reality; Kull of Atlantis sits enthroned in ancient Valusia.

THE SHADOW KINGDOM

1. A King Comes Riding

The blare of the trumpets grew louder, like a deep golden tide surge, like the soft booming of the evening tides against the silver beaches of Valusia. The throng shouted, women flung roses from the roofs as the rhythmic chiming of silver hoofs came clearer and the first of the mighty array swung into view in the broad white street that curved round the golden-spired Tower of Splendor.

First came the trumpeters, slim youths, clad in scarlet, riding with a flourish of long, slender golden trumpets; next the bowmen, tall men from the mountains; and behind these the heavily armed footmen, their broad shields clashing in unison, their long spears swaying in perfect rhythm to their stride. Behind them came the mightiest soldiery in all the world, the Red Slayers, horsemen, splendidly mounted, armed in red from helmet to spur. Proudly they sat their steeds, looking neither to right nor to left, but aware of the shouting for all that. Like bronze statues they were, and there was never a waver in the forest of spears that reared above them.

Behind those proud and terrible ranks came the motley files of the mercenaries, fierce, wild-looking warriors, men of Mu and of Kaa-u and of the hills of the east and the isles of the west. They bore spears and heavy swords, and a compact group that marched somewhat apart were the bowmen of Lemuria. Then came the light foot of the nation, and more trumpeters brought up the rear.

A brave sight, and a sight which aroused a fierce thrill in the soul of Kull, king of Valusia. Not on the Topaz Throne at the front of the regal Tower of Splendor sat Kull, but in the saddle, mounted on a great stallion, a true warrior king. His mighty arm swung up in reply to the salutes as the hosts passed. His fierce eyes passed the gorgeous trumpeters with a casual glance, rested longer on the following soldiery; they blazed with a ferocious light as the Red Slayers halted in front of him with a clang of arms and a rearing of steeds, and tendered him the crown salute. They narrowed slightly as the mercenaries strode by. They saluted no one, the mercenaries. They walked with shoulders flung back, eyeing Kull boldly and straightly, albeit with a certain appreciation; fierce eyes, unblinking; savage eyes, staring from beneath shaggy manes and heavy brows.

And Kull gave back a like stare. He granted much to brave men, and there were no braver in all the world, not even among the wild tribesmen who now disowned him. But Kull was too much the savage to have any great love for these. There were too many feuds. Many were age-old enemies of Kull's nation, and though the name of Kull was now a word accursed among the mountains and valleys of his people, and though Kull had put them from his mind, yet the old hates, the ancient passions still lingered. For Kull was no Valusian but an Atlantean.

The armies swung out of sight around the gem-blazing shoulders of the Tower of Splendor and Kull reined his stallion about and started toward the palace at an easy gait, discussing the review with the commanders that rode with him, using not many words, but saying much.

"The army is like a sword," said Kull, "and must not be allowed to rust." So down the street they rode, and

Kull gave no heed to any of the whispers that reached his hearing from the throngs that still swarmed the streets.

"That is Kull, see! Valka! But what a king! And what a man! Look at his arms! His shoulders!"

And an undertone of more sinister whisperings: "Kull! Ha, accursed usurper from the pagan isles"—"Aye, shame to Valusia that a barbarian sits on the Throne of Kings.". . .

Little did Kull heed. Heavyhanded had he seized the decaying throne of ancient Valusia and with a heavier hand did he hold it, a man against a nation.

After the council chamber, the social palace where Kull replied to the formal and laudatory phrases of the lords and ladies, with carefully hidden, grim amusement at such frivolities; then the lords and ladies took their formal departure and Kull leaned back upon the ermine throne and contemplated matters of state until an attendant requested permission from the great king to speak, and announced an emissary from the Pictish embassy.

Kull brought his mind back from the dim mazes of Valusian statecraft where it had been wandering, and gazed upon the Pict with little favor. The man gave back the gaze of the king without flinching. He was a lean-hipped, massive-chested warrior of middle height, dark, like all his race, and strongly built. From strong, immobile features gazed dauntless and inscrutable eyes.

"The chief of the Councilors, Ka-nu of the tribe, right hand of the king of Pictdom, sends greetings and says: 'There is a throne at the feast of the rising moon for Kull, king of kings, lord of lords, emperor of Valusia.' "

"Good," answered Kull. "Say to Ka-nu the Ancient, ambassador of the western isles, that the king of Valusia will quaff wine with him when the moon floats over the hills of Zalgara."

Still the Pict lingered. "I have a word for the king, not"—with a contemptuous flirt of his hand—"for these slaves."

Kull dismissed the attendants with a word, watching the Pict warily.

The man stepped nearer, and lowered his voice: "Come alone to feast tonight, lord king. Such was the word of my chief."

The king's eyes narrowed, gleaming like gray sword steel, coldly.

"Alone?"

"Aye."

They eyed each other silently, their mutual tribal enmity seething beneath their cloak of formality. Their mouths spoke the cultured speech, the conventional court phrases of a highly polished race, a race not their own, but from their eyes gleamed the primal traditions of the elemental savage. Kull might be the king of Valusia and the Pict might be an emissary to her courts, but there in the throne hall of kings, two tribesmen glowered at each other, fierce and wary, while ghosts of wild wars and world-ancient feuds whispered to each.

To the king was the advantage and he enjoyed it to its fullest extent. Jaw resting on hand, he eyed the Pict, who stood like an image of bronze, head flung back, eyes unflinching.

Across Kull's lips stole a smile that was more a sneer.

"And so I am to come—alone?" Civilization had taught him to speak by innuendo and the Pict's dark eyes glittered, though he made no reply. "How am I to know that you come from Ka-nu?"

"I have spoken," was the sullen response.

"And when did a Pict speak truth?" sneered Kull, fully aware that the Picts never lied, but using this means to enrage the man.

"I see your plan, king," the Pict answered imperturbably. "You wish to anger me. By Valka, you need go no further! I am angry enough. And I challenge you to meet me in single battle, spear, sword or dagger, mounted or afoot. Are you king or man?"

Kull's eyes glinted with the grudging admiration a

warrior must needs give a bold foeman, but he did not fail to use the chance of further annoying his antagonist.

"A king does not accept the challenge of a nameless savage," he sneered, "nor does the emperor of Valusia break the Truce of Ambassadors. You have leave to go. Say to Ka-nu that I will come alone."

The Pict's eyes flashed murderously. He fairly shook in the grasp of the primitive blood-lust; then, turning his back squarely upon the king of Valusia, he strode across the Hall of Society and vanished through the great door.

Again Kull leaned back upon the ermine throne and meditated.

So the chief of the Council of Picts wished him to come alone? But for what reason? Treachery? Grimly Kull touched the hilt of his great sword. But scarcely. The Picts valued too greatly the alliance with Valusia to break it for any feudal reason. Kull might be a warrior of Atlantis and hereditary enemy of all Picts, but too, he was king of Valusia, the most potent ally of the Men of the West.

Kull reflected long upon the strange state of affairs that made him ally of ancient foes and foe of ancient friends. He rose and paced restlessly across the hall, with the quick, noiseless tread of a lion. Chains of friendship, tribe and tradition had he broken to satisfy his ambition. And, by Valka, god of the sea and the land, he had realized that ambition! He was king of Valusia—a fading, degenerate Valusia, a Valusia living mostly in dreams of bygone glory, but still a mighty land and the greatest of the Seven Empires. Valusia—Land of Dreams, the tribesmen named it, and sometimes it seemed to Kull that he moved in a dream. Strange to him were the intrigues of court and palace, army and people. All was like a masquerade, where men and women hid their real thoughts with a smooth mask. Yet the seizing of the throne had been easy—a bold snatching of opportunity, the swift whirl of swords, the slaying of a tyrant of whom men had wearied unto death, short, crafty plotting with ambitious statesmen out of favor at court—and Kull, wandering adventurer, Atlantean exile, had swept up to the dizzy heights of his dreams: he was lord of Valusia, king of kings. Yet now it seemed that the seizing was far easier than the keeping. The sight of the Pict had brought back youthful associations to his mind, the free, wild savagery of his boyhood. And now a strange feeling of dim unrest, of unreality, stole over him as of late it had been doing. Who was he, a straightforward man of the seas and the mountain, to rule a race strangely and terribly wise with the mysticisms of antiquity? An ancient race—

"I am Kull!" said he, flinging back his head as a lion flings back his mane. "I am Kull!"

His falcon gaze swept the ancient hall. His self-confidence flowed back. . . . And in a dim nook of the hall a tapestry moved—slightly.

2. Thus Spake the Silent Halls of Valusia

The moon had not risen, and the garden was lighted with torches aglow in silver cressets when Kull sat down on the throne before the table of Ka-nu, ambassador of the western isles. At his right hand sat the ancient Pict, as much unlike an emissary of that fierce race as a man could be. Ancient was Ka-nu and wise in statecraft, grown old in the game. There was no elemental hatred in the eyes that looked at Kull appraisingly; no Tribal traditions hindered his judgments. Long associations with the statesmen of the civilized nations had swept away such cobwebs. Not: who and what is this man? was the question ever foremost in Ka-nu's mind, but: can I use this man, and how? Tribal prejudices he used only to further his own schemes.

And Kull watched Ka-nu, answering his conversation briefly, wondering if civilization would make of him a thing like the Pict. For Ka-nu was soft and paunchy. Many years had stridden across the sky-rim since Ka-nu had wielded a sword. True, he was old, but Kull had seen men older than he in the forefront of battle. The Picts were a long-lived race. A beautiful girl stood at Ka-nu's elbow, refilling his goblet, and she was kept busy. Meanwhile Ka-nu kept up a running fire of jests and comments, and Kull, secretly contemptuous of his garrulity, nevertheless missed none of his shrewd humor.

At the banquet were Pictish chiefs and statesmen, the latter jovial and easy in their manner, the warriors formally courteous, but plainly hampered by their tribal affinities. Yet Kull, with a tinge of envy, was cognizant of the freedom and ease of the affair as contrasted with like affairs of the Valusian court. Such freedom prevailed in the rude camps of Atlantis—Kull shrugged his shoulders. After all, doubtless Ka-nu, who had seemed to have forgotten he was a Pict as far as time-hoary custom and prejudice went, was right and he, Kull, would better become a Valusian in mind as in name.

At last when the moon had reached her zenith, Ka-nu, having eaten and drunk as much as any three men there, leaned back upon his divan with a comfortable sigh and said, "Now, get you gone, friends, for the king and I would converse on such matters as concern not children. Yes, you too, my pretty; yet first let me kiss those ruby lips—so; no, dance away, my rose-bloom."

Ka-nu's eyes twinkled above his white beard as he surveyed Kull, who sat erect, grim and uncompromising.

"You are thinking, Kull," said the old statesman, suddenly, "that Ka-nu is a useless old reprobate, fit for nothing except to guzzle wine and kiss wenches!"

In fact, this remark was so much in line with his actual thoughts, and so plainly put, that Kull was rather startled, though he gave no sign.

Ka-nu gurgled and his paunch shook with his mirth. "Wine is red and women are soft," he remarked tolerantly. "But—ha! ha!—think not old Ka-nu allows either to interfere with business."

Again he laughed, and Kull moved restlessly. This seemed much like being made sport of, and the king's scintillant eyes began to glow with a feline light.

Ka-nu reached for the wine-pitcher, filled his beaker and glanced questioningly at Kull, who shook his head irritably.

"Aye," said Ka-nu equably, "it takes an old head to stand strong drink. I am growing old, Kull, so why should you young men begrudge me such pleasures as we old-sters must find? Ah me, I grow ancient and withered, friendless and cheerless."

But his looks and expressions failed far of bearing out his words. His rubicund countenance fairly glowed, and his eyes sparkled, so that his white beard seemed incongruous. Indeed, he looked remarkably elfin, reflected Kull, who felt vaguely resentful. The old scoundrel had lost all of the primitive virtues of his race and of Kull's race, yet he seemed more pleased in his aged days than otherwise.

"Hark ye, Kull," said Ka-nu, raising an admonitory finger, "'tis a chancy thing to laud a young man, yet I must speak my true thoughts to gain your confidence."

"If you think to gain it by flattery—"

"Tush. Who spake of flattery? I flatter only to disguard."

There was a keen sparkle in Ka-nu's eyes, a cold glimmer that did not match his lazy smile. He knew men, and he knew that to gain his end he must smite straight with this tigerish barbarian, who, like a wolf scenting a snare, would scent out unerringly any falseness in the skein of his wordweb.

"You have power, Kull," said he, choosing his words with more care than he did in the council rooms of the nation, "to make yourself mightiest of all kings, and restore some of the lost glories of Valusia. So. I care little for Valusia—though the women and wine be excellent—save for the fact that the stronger Valusia is, the stronger is the Pict nation. More, with an Atlantean on the throne, eventually Atlantis will become united—"

Kull laughed in harsh mockery. Ka-nu had touched an old wound.

"Atlantis made my name accursed when I went to seek fame and fortune among the cities of the world. We—they—are age-old foes of the Seven Empires, greater foes of the allies of the Empires, as you should know."

Ka-nu tugged his beard and smiled enigmatically.

"Nay, nay. Let it pass. But I know whereof I speak. And then warfare will cease, wherein there is no gain; I see a world of peace and prosperity—man loving his fellow man—the good supreme. All this can you accomplish—*if you live!*"

"Ha!" Kull's lean hand closed on his hilt and he half rose, with a sudden movement of such dynamic speed that Ka-nu, who fancied men as some men fancy blooded horses, felt his old blood leap with a sudden thrill. Valka, what a warrior! Nerves and sinews of steel and fire, bound together with the perfect co-ordination, the fighting instinct, that makes the terrible warrior.

But none of Ka-nu's enthusiasm showed in his mildly sarcastic tone.

"Tush. Be seated. Look about you. The gardens are deserted, the seats empty, save for ourselves. You fear not *me?*"

Kull sank back, gazing about him warily.

"There speaks the savage," mused Ka-nu. "Think you if I planned treachery I would enact it here where suspicion would be sure to fall upon me? Tut. You young tribesmen have much to learn. There were my chiefs who were not at ease because you were born among the hills of Atlantis, and you despise me in your secret mind because I am a Pict. Tush. I see you as Kull, king of Valusia, not as Kull, the reckless Atlantean, leader of the raiders who harried the western isles. So you should see in me, not a Pict but an international man, a figure of the world. Now to that figure, hark! If you were slain tomorrow who would be king?"

"Kaanuub, baron of Blaal."

"Even so. I object to Kaanuub for many reasons, yet most of all for the fact that he is but a figurehead."

"How so? He was my greatest opponent, but I did not know that he championed any cause but his own."

"The night can hear," answered Ka-nu obliquely. "There are worlds within worlds. But you may trust me and you may trust Brule, the Spear-slayer. Look!" He drew from his robes a bracelet of gold representing a winged dragon coiled thrice, with three horns of ruby on the head.

"Examine it closely. Brule will wear it on his arm when he comes to you tomorrow night so that you may know him. Trust Brule as you trust yourself, and do what he tells you to. And in proof of trust, look ye!"

And with the speed of a striking hawk, the ancient snatched something from his robes, something that flung a weird green light over them, and which he replaced in an instant.

"The stolen gem!" exclaimed Kull recoiling. "The green jewel from the Temple of the Serpent! Valka! You! And why do you show it to me?"

"To save your life. To prove my trust. If I betray your trust, deal with me likewise. You hold my life in your hand. Now I could not be false to you if I would, for a word from you would be my doom."

Yet for all his words the old scoundrel beamed merrily and seemed vastly pleased with himself.

"But why do you give me this hold over you?" asked Kull, becoming more bewildered each second.

"As I told you. Now, you see that I do not intend to deal you false, and tomorrow night when Brule comes to you, you will follow his advice without fear of treachery. Enough. An escort waits outside to ride to the palace with you, lord."

Kull rose. "But you have told me nothing."

"Tush. How impatient are youths!" Ka-nu looked more like a mischievous elf than ever. "Go you and dream of thrones and power and kingdoms, while I dream of wine and soft women and roses. And fortune ride with you, King Kull."

As he left the garden, Kull glanced back to see Ka-nu still reclining lazily in his seat, a merry ancient, beaming on all the world with jovial fellowship.

A mounted warrior waited for the king just without the garden and Kull was slightly surprised to see that it was the same that had brought Ka-nu's invitation. No word was spoken as Kull swung into the saddle nor as they clattered along the empty streets.

The color and the gayety of the day had given way to the eerie stillness of night. The city's antiquity was more than ever apparent beneath the bent, silver moon. The huge pillars of the mansions and palaces towered up into the stars. The broad stairways, silent and deserted, seemed to climb endlessly until they vanished in the shadowy darkness of the upper realms. Stairs to the stars, thought Kull, his imaginative mind inspired by the weird grandeur of the scene.

Clang! clang! clang! sounded the silver hoofs on the broad, moon-flooded streets, but otherwise there was no sound. The age of the city, its incredible antiquity, was almost oppressive to the king; it was as if the great silent buildings laughed at him, noiselessly, with unguessable mockery. And what secrets did they hold?

"You are young," said the palaces and the temples and the shrines, "but we are old. The world was wild with youth when we were reared. You and your tribe shall pass, but we are invincible, indestructible. We towered above a strange world, ere Atlantis and Lemuria rose from the sea; we still shall reign when the green waters sigh for many a restless fathom above the spires of Lemuria and the hills of Atlantis and when the isles of the Western Men are the mountains of a strange land.

"How many kings have we watched ride down these streets before Kull of Atlantis was even a dream in the mind of Ka, bird of Creation? Ride on, Kull of Atlantis; greater shall follow you; greater came before you. They are dust; they are forgotten; we stand; we know; we are. Ride, ride on, Kull of Atlantis; Kull the king, Kull the fool!"

And it seemed to Kull that the clashing hoofs took up the silent refrain to beat it into the night with hollow re-echoing mockery:

"Kull—the—king! Kull—the—fool!"

Glow, moon; you light a king's way! Gleam, stars; you are torches in the train of an emperor! And clang, silver-shod hoofs; you herald that Kull rides through Valusia.

Ho! Awake, Valusia! It is Kull that rides, Kull the king!

"We have known many kings," said the silent halls of Valusia.

And so in a brooding mood Kull came to the palace, where his bodyguard, men of the Red Slayers, came to take the rein of the great stallion and escort Kull to his rest. There the Pict, still sullenly speechless, wheeled his steed with a savage wrench of the rein and fled away in the dark like a phantom; Kull's heightened imagination pictured him speeding through the silent streets like a goblin out of the Elder World.

There was no sleep for Kull that night, for it was nearly dawn and he spent the rest of the night hours pacing the throneroom, and pondering over what had passed. Ka-nu had told him nothing, yet he had put himself in Kull's complete power. At what had he hinted when he had said the baron of Blaal was naught but a figurehead? And who was this Brule who was to come to him by night, wearing the mystic armlet of the dragon? And why? Above all, why had Ka-nu shown him the green gem of terror, stolen long ago from the temple of the Serpent, for which the world would rock in wars were it known to the weird and terrible keepers of that temple, and from whose vengeance not even Ka-nu's ferocious tribesmen might be able to save him? But Ka-nu knew he was safe, reflected Kull, for the statesman was too shrewd to expose himself to risk without profit. But was it to throw the king off his guard and pave the way to treachery? Would Ka-nu dare let him live now? Kull shrugged his shoulders.

3. They That Walk the Night

The moon had not risen when Kull, hand to hilt, stepped to a window. The windows opened upon the great inner gardens of the royal palace, and the breezes of the night, bearing the scents of spice trees, blew the filmy curtains about. The king looked out. The walks and groves were deserted; carefully trimmed trees were bulky shadows; fountains near by flung their slender sheen of silver in the starlight and distant fountains rippled steadily. No guards walked those gardens, for so closely were the outer walls guarded that it seemed impossible for any invader to gain access to them.

Vines curled up the walls of the palace, and even as Kull mused upon the ease with which they might be climbed, a segment of shadow detached itself from the darkness below the window and a bare, brown arm curved up over the sill. Kull's great sword hissed halfway from the sheath; then the king halted. Upon the muscular forearm gleamed the dragon armlet shown him by Ka-nu the night before.

The possessor of the arm pulled himself up over the sill and into the room with the swift, easy motion of a climbing leopard.

"You are Brule?" asked Kull, and then stopped in surprise not unmingled with annoyance and suspicion; for the man was he whom Kull had taunted in the Hall of Society; the same who had escorted him from the Pictish embassy.

"I am Brule, the Spear-slayer," answered the Pict in a guarded voice; then swiftly, gazing closely in Kull's face, he said, barely above a whisper:

"Ka nama kaa lajerama!"

Kull started. "Ha! What mean you?"

"Know you not?"

"Nay, the words are unfamiliar; they are of no language I ever heard—and yet, by Valka!—somewhere—I have heard—"

"Aye," was the Pict's only comment. His eyes swept the room, the study room of the palace. Except for a few tables, a divan or two and great shelves of books of parchment, the room was barren compared to the grandeur of the rest of the palace.

"Tell me, king, who guards the door?"

"Eighteen of the Red Slayers. But how come you, stealing through the gardens by night and scaling the walls of the palace?"

Brule sneered. "The guards of Valusia are blind buffaloes. I could steal their girls from under their noses. I stole amid them and they saw me not nor heard me. And the walls—I could scale them without the aid of vines. I have hunted tigers on the foggy beaches when the sharp east breezes blew the mist in from seaward and I have climbed the steeps of the western sea mountain. But come—nay, touch this armlet."

He held out his arm and, as Kull complied wonderingly, gave an apparent sigh of relief.

"So. Now throw off those kingly robes; for there are ahead of you this night such deeds as no Atlantean ever dreamed of."

Brule himself was clad only in a scanty loin-cloth through which was thrust a short, curved sword.

"And who are you to give me orders?" asked Kull, slightly resentful.

"Did not Ka-nu bid you follow me in all things?" asked the Pict irritably, his eyes flashing momentarily. "I have no love for you, lord, but for the moment I have put the thought of feuds from my mind. Do you likewise. But come."

Walking noiselessly, he led the way across the room to the door. A slide in the door allowed a view of the outer corridor, unseen from without, and the Pict bade Kull look.

"What see you?"

"Naught but the eighteen guardsmen."

The Pict nodded, motioned Kull to follow him across the room. At a panel in the opposite wall Brule stopped and fumbled there a moment. Then with a light movement he stepped back, drawing his sword as he did so. Kull gave an exclamation as the panel swung silently open, revealing a dimly lighted passageway.

"A secret passage!" swore Kull softly. "And I knew nothing of it! By Valka, someone shall dance for this!"

"Silence!" hissed the Pict.

Brule was standing like a bronze statue as if straining every nerve for the slightest sound; something about his attitude made Kull's hair prickle slightly, not from fear but from some eery anticipation. Then beckoning, Brule stepped through the secret doorway which stood open behind them. The passage was bare, but not dust-covered as should have been the case with an unused secret corridor. A vague, gray light filtered through somewhere, but the source of it was not apparent. Every few feet Kull saw doors, invisible, as he knew, from the outside, but easily apparent from within.

"The palace is a very honeycomb," he muttered.

"Aye. Night and day you are watched, king, by many eyes."

The king was impressed by Brule's manner. The Pict went forward slowly, warily, half crouching, blade held low and thrust forward. When he spoke it was in a whisper and he continually flung glances from side to side.

The corridor turned sharply and Brule warily gazed past the turn.

"Look!" he whispered. "But remember! No word! No sound—on your life!"

Kull cautiously gazed past him. The corridor changed just at the bend to a flight of steps. And then Kull recoiled. At the foot of those stairs lay the eighteen Red Slayers who were that night stationed to watch the king's study room. Brule's grip upon his mighty arm and Brule's fierce whisper at his shoulder alone kept Kull from leaping down those stairs.

"Silent, Kull! Silent, in Valka's name!" hissed the Pict. "These corridors are empty now, but I risked much in showing you, that you might then believe what I had to say. Back now to the room of study." And he retraced his steps, Kull following; his mind in a turmoil of bewilderment.

"This is treachery," muttered the king, his steel-gray eyes a-smolder, "foul and swift! Mere minutes have passed since those men stood at guard."

Again in the room of study Brule carefully closed the secret panel and motioned Kull to look again through the slit of the outer door. Kull gasped audibly. *For without stood the eighteen guardsmen!*

"This is sorcery!" he whispered, half-drawing his sword. "Do dead men guard the king?"

"*Aye!*" came Brule's scarcely audible reply; there was a strange expression in the Pict's scintillant eyes. They looked squarely into each other's eyes for an instant, Kull's brow wrinkled in a puzzled scowl as he strove to read the Pict's inscrutable face. Then Brule's lips, barely moving, formed the words:

"*The—snake—that—speaks!*"

"Silent!" whispered Kull, laying his hand over Brule's mouth. "That is death to speak! That is a name accursed!"

The Pict's fearless eyes regarded him steadily.

"Look, again, King Kull. Perchance the guard was changed."

"Nay, those are the same men. In Valka's name, this

is sorcery—this is insanity! I saw with my own eyes the bodies of those men, not eight minutes agone. Yet there they stand."

Brule stepped back, away from the door, Kull mechanically following.

"Kull, what know ye of the traditions of this race ye rule?"

"Much—and yet, little. Valusia is so old—"

"Aye," Brule's eyes lighted strangely, "we are but barbarians—infants compared to the Seven Empires. Not even they themselves know how old they are. Neither the memory of man nor the annals of the historians reach back far enough to tell us when the first men came up from the sea and built cities on the shore. But Kull, *men were not always ruled by men!*"

The king started. Their eyes met.

"Aye, there is a legend of my people—"

"And mine!" broke in Brule. "That was before we of the isles were allied with Valusia. Aye, in the reign of Lion-fang, seventh war chief of the Picts, so many years ago no man remembers how many. Across the sea we came, from the isles of the sunset, skirting the shores of Atlantis, and falling upon the beaches of Valusia with fire and sword. Aye, the long white beaches resounded with the clash of spears, and the night was like day from the flame of the burning castles. And the king, the king of Valusia, who died on the red sea sands that dim day—" His voice trailed off; the two stared at each other, neither speaking; then each nodded.

"Ancient is Valusia!" whispered Kull. "The hills of Atlantis and Mu were isles of the sea when Valusia was young."

The night breeze whispered through the open window. Not the free, crisp sea air such as Brule and Kull knew and reveled in, in their land, but a breath like a whisper from the past, laden with musk, scents of forgotten things, breathing secrets that were hoary when the world was young.

The tapestries rustled, and suddenly Kull felt like a naked child before the inscrutable wisdom of the mystic past. Again the sense of unreality swept upon him. At the back of his soul stole dim, gigantic phantoms, whispering monstrous things. He sensed that Brule experienced similar thoughts. The Pict's eyes were fixed upon his face with a fierce intensity. Their glances met. Kull felt warmly a sense of comradeship with this member of an enemy tribe. Like rival leopards turning at bay against hunters, these two savages made common cause against the inhuman powers of antiquity.

Brule again led the way back to the secret door. Silently they entered and silently they proceeded down the dim corridor, taking the opposite direction from that in which they previously traversed it. After a while the Pict stopped and pressed close to one of the secret doors, bidding Kull look with him through the hidden slot.

" This opens upon a little-used stair which leads to a corridor running past the study-room door."

They gazed, and presently, mounting the stair silently, came a silent shape.

" Tu! Chief eouncilor!" exclaimed Kull. "By night and with bared dagger! How, what means this, Brule?"

"Murder! And foulest treachery!" hissed Brule. "Nay"—as Kull would have flung the door aside and leaped forth—"we are lost if you meet him here, for more lurk at the foot of those stairs. Come!"

Half running, they darted back along the passage. Back through the secret door Brule led, shutting it carefully behind them, then across the chamber to an opening into a room seldom used. There he swept aside some tapestries in a dim corner nook and, drawing Kull with him, stepped behind them. Minutes dragged. Kull could hear the breeze in the other room blowing the window curtains about, and it seemed to him like the murmur of ghosts. Then through the door, stealthily, came Tu, chief councilor of the king. Evidently he had come through the study room and, finding it empty, sought his victim where he was most likely to be.

He came with upraised dagger, walking silently. A moment he halted, gazing about the apparently empty room, which was lighted dimly by a single candle. Then he advanced cautiously, apparently at a loss to understand the absence of the king. He stood before the hiding place—and—

"Slay!" hissed the Pict.

Kull with a single mighty leap hurled himself into the room. Tu spun, but the blinding, tigerish speed of the attack gave him no chance for defense or counter-attack. Sword steel flashed in the dim light and grated on bone as Tu toppled backward, Kull's sword standing out between his shoulders.

Kull leaned above him, teeth bared in the killer's snarl, heavy brows a-scowl above eyes that were like the gray ice of the cold sea. Then he released the hilt and recoiled, shaken, dizzy, the hand of death at his spine.

For as he watched, Tu's face became strangely dim and unreal; the features mingled and merged in a seemingly impossible manner. Then, like a fading mask of fog, the face suddenly vanished and in its stead gaped and leered a *monstrous serpent's head!*

"Valka!" gasped Kull, sweat beading his forehead, and again: "Valka!"

Brule leaned forward, face immobile. Yet his glittering eyes mirrored something of Kull's horror.

"Regain your sword, lord king," said he. "There are yet deeds to be done."

Hesitantly Kull set his hand to the hilt. His flesh crawled as he set his foot upon the terror which lay at their feet, and as some jerk of muscular reaction caused the frightful mouth to gape suddenly, he recoiled, weak with nausea. Then, wrathful at himself, he plucked forth his sword and gazed more closely at the nameless thing that had been known as Tu, chief councilor. Save for the reptilian head, the thing was the exact counterpart of a man.

"A man with the head of a snake!" Kull murmured. "This, then, is a priest of the serpent god?"

"Aye. Tu sleeps unknowing. These fiends can take any form they will. That is, they can, by a magic charm or the like, fling a web of sorcery about their faces, as an actor dons a mask, so that they resemble anyone they wish to."

"Then the old legends were true," mused the king; "the grim old tales few dare even whisper, lest they die as blasphemers, are no fantasies. By Valka, I had thought—I had guessed—but it seems beyond the bounds of reality. Ha! The guardsmen outside the door—"

"They too are snake-men. Hold! What would you do?"

"Slay them!" said Kull between his teeth.

"Strike at the skull if at all," said Brule. "Eighteen wait without the door and perhaps a score more in the corridors. Hark ye, king, Ka-nu learned of this plot. His spies have pierced the inmost fastnesses of the snake priests and they brought hints of a plot. Long ago he discovered the secret passageways of the palace, and at his command I studied the map thereof and came here by night to aid you, lest you die as other kings of Valusia have died. I came alone for the reason that to send more would have roused suspicion. Many could not steal into the palace as I did. Some of the foul conspiracy you have seen. Snake-men guard your door, and that one, as Tu, could pass anywhere else in the palace; in the morning, if the priests failed, the real guards would be holding their places again, nothing knowing, nothing remembering; there to take the blame if the priests succeeded. But stay you here while I dispose of this carrion."

So saying, the Pict shouldered the frightful thing stolidly and vanished with it through another secret panel. Kull stood alone, his mind a-whirl. Neophytes of the mighty serpent, how many lurked among his cities? How might he tell the false from the true? Aye, how many of his trusted councilors, his generals, were men? He could be certain—of whom?

The secret panel swung inward and Brule entered.

"You were swift."

"Aye!" The warrior stepped forward, eyeing the floor. "There is gore upon the rug. See?"

Kull bent forward; from the corner of his eye he saw a blur of movement, a glint of steel. Like a loosened bow he whipped erect, thrusting upward. The warrior sagged upon the sword, his own clattering to the floor. Even at that instant Kull reflected grimly that it was appropriate that the traitor should meet his death upon the sliding, upward thrust used so much by his race. Then, as Brule slid from the sword to sprawl motionless on the floor, the face began to merge and fade, and as Kull caught his breath, his hair a-prickle, the human features vanished and there the jaws of a great snake gaped hideously, the terrible beady eyes venomous even in death.

"He was a snake priest all the time!" gasped the king. "Valka! What an elaborate plan to throw me off my guard! Ka-nu there, is he a man? Was it Ka-nu to whom I talked in the gardens? Almighty Valka!" as his flesh crawled with a horrid thought; "are the people of Valusia men or are they *all* serpents?"

Undecided he stood, idly seeing that the thing named Brule no longer wore the dragon armlet. A sound made him wheel.

Brule was coming through the secret door.

"Hold!" Upon the arm upthrown to halt the king's hovering sword gleamed the dragon armlet. "Valka!" The Pict stopped short. Then a grim smile curled his lips.

"By the gods of the seas! These demons are crafty past reckoning. For it must be that one lurked in the corridors, and seeing me go carrying the carcass of that other, took my appearance. So. I have another to do away with."

"Hold!" There was the menace of death in Kull's voice;

"I have seen two men turn to serpents before my eyes. How may I know if you are a true man?"

Brule laughed. "For two reasons, King Kull. No snake-man wears this"—he indicated the dragon armlet—"nor can any say these words," and again Kull heard the strange phrase: *"Ka nama kaa lajerama."*

"Ka nama kaa lajerama," Kull repeated mechanically. "Now, where, in Valka's name, have I heard that? I have not! And yet—and yet—"

"Aye, you remember, Kull," said Brule. "Through the dim corridors of memory those words lurk; though you never heard them in this life, yet in the bygone ages they were so terribly impressed upon the soul mind that never dies, that they will always strike dim chords in your memory, though you be reincarnated for a million years to come. For that phrase has come secretly down the grim and bloody eons, since when, uncounted centuries ago, those words were watchwords for the race of men who battled with the grisly beings of the Elder Universe. For none but a real man of men may speak them, whose jaws and mouth are shaped different from any other creature. Their meaning has been forgotten but not the words themselves."

"True," said Kull. "I remember the legends—Valka!" He stopped short, staring, for suddenly, like the silent swinging wide of a mystic door, misty, unfathomed reaches opened in the recesses of his consciousness and for an instant he seemed to gaze back through the vastness that spanned life and life; seeing through the vague and ghostly fogs dim shapes reliving dead centuries— men in combat with hideous monsters, vanquishing a planet of frightful terrors. Against a gray, ever-shifting background moved strange nightmare forms, fantasies of lunacy and fear; and man, the jest of the gods, the blind, wisdomless striver from dust to dust, following the long bloody trail of his destiny, knowing not why, bestial, blundering, like a great murderous child, yet feeling somewhere a spark of divine fire. . . . Kull drew a hand across his brow, shaken; these sudden glimpses into the abysses of memory always startled him.

"They are gone," said Brule, as if scanning his secret mind; "the bird-women, the harpies, the bat-men, the flying fiends, the wolf-people, the demons, the goblins— all save such as this being that lies at our feet, and a few of the wolf-men. Long and terrible was the war, lasting through the bloody centuries, since first the first men, risen from the mire of apedom, turned upon those who then ruled the world. And at last mankind conquered, so long ago that naught but dim legends come to us through the ages. The snake-people were the last to go, yet at last men conquered even them and drove them forth into the waste lands of the world, there to mate with true snakes until some day, say the sages, the horrid breed shall vanish utterly. Yet the Things returned in crafty guise as men grew soft and degenerate, forgetting ancient wars. Ah, that was a grim and secret war! Among the men of the Younger Earth stole the frightful monsters of the Elder Planet, safeguarded by their horrid wisdom and mysticisms, taking all forms and shapes, doing deeds of horror secretly. No man knew who was true man and who false. No man could trust any man. Yet by means of their own craft they formed ways by which the false might be known from the true. Men took for a sign and a standard the figure of the flying dragon, the winged dinosaur, a monster of past ages, which was the greatest foe of the serpent. And men used those words which I spoke to you as a sign and symbol, for as I said, none but a true man can repeat them. So mankind triumphed. Yet again the fiends came after the years of forgetfulness had gone by—for man is still an ape in that he forgets what is not ever before his eyes. As priests they came; and for that men in their luxury and might had by then lost faith in the old religions and worships, the snake-men, in the guise of teachers of a new and truer cult, built a monstrous religion about the worship of the serpent god. Such is their power that it is now death to repeat the old legends of the snake-people, and people bow again to the serpent god in new form; and blind fools that they are, the great hosts of men see no connection between this power and the power men overthrew eons ago. As priests the snake-men are content to rule—and yet—" He stopped.

"Go on." Kull felt an unaccountable stirring of the short hair at the base of his scalp.

"Kings have reigned as true men in Valusia," the Pict whispered, "and yet, slain in battle, have died serpents— as died he who fell beneath the spear of Lion-fang on the red beaches when we of the isles harried the Seven Empires. And how can this be, Lord Kull? These kings were born of women and lived as men! This—the true kings died in secret—as you would have died tonight— and priests of the Serpent reigned in their stead, no man knowing."

Kull cursed between his teeth. "Aye, it must be. No one has ever seen a priest of the Serpent and lived, that is known. They live in utmost secrecy."

"The statecraft of the Seven Empires is a mazy, monstrous thing," said Brule. "There the true men know that among them glide the spies of the Serpent, and the men who are the Serpent's allies—such as Kaanuub, baron of Blaal—yet no man dares seek to unmask a suspect lest vengeance befall him. No man trusts his fellow and the true statesmen dare not speak to each other what is in the minds of all. Could they be sure, could a snake-man or plot be unmasked before them all, then would the power of the Serpent be more than half broken; for all would then ally and make common cause, sifting out the traitors. Ka-nu alone is of sufficient shrewdness and courage to cope with them, and even Ka-nu learned only enough of their plot to tell me what would happen— what has happened up to this time. Thus far I was prepared; from now on we must trust to our luck and our craft. Here and now I think we are safe; those snake-men without the door dare not leave their post lest true men come here unexpectedly. But tomorrow they will try something else, you may be sure. Just what they will do, none can say, not even Ka-nu; but we must stay at each other's sides, King Kull, until we conquer or both be dead. Now come with me while I take this carcass to the hiding-place where I took the other being."

Kull followed the Pict with his grisly burden through the secret panel and down the dim corridor. Their feet, trained to the silence of the wilderness, made no noise. Like phantoms they glided through the ghostly light, Kull wondering that the corridors should be deserted; at every turn he expected to run full upon some frightful apparition. Suspicion surged back upon him; was this Pict leading him into ambush? He fell back a pace or two behind Brule, his ready sword hovering at the Pict's unheeding back. Brule should die first if he meant treachery. But if the Pict was aware of the king's suspicion, he showed no sign. Stolidly he tramped along, until they came to a room, dusty and long unused, where moldy tapestries hung heavy. Brule drew aside some of these and concealed the corpse behind them.

Then they turned to retrace their steps, when suddenly Brule halted with such abruptness that he was closer to death than he knew; for Kull's nerves were on edge.

"Something moving in the corridor," hissed the Pict. "Ka-nu said these ways would be empty, yet—"

He drew his sword and stole into the corridor, Kull following warily.

A short way down the corridor a strange, vague glow appeared that came toward them. Nerves a-leap, they waited, backs to the corridor wall; for what they knew not, but Kull heard Brule's breath hiss through his teeth and was reassured as to Brule's loyalty.

The glow merged into a shadowy form. A shape vaguely like a man it was, but misty and illusive, like a wisp of fog, that grew more tangible as it approached, but never fully material. A face looked at them, a pair of luminous great eyes, that seemed to hold all the tortures of a million centuries. There was no menace in that face, with its dim, worn features, but only a great pity—and that face—that face—

"Almighty gods!" breathed Kull, an icy hand at his soul; "Eallal, king of Valusia, who died a thousand years ago!"

Brule shrank back as far as he could, his narrow eyes widened in a blaze of pure horror, the sword shaking in his grip, unnerved for the first time that weird night. Erect and defiant stood Kull, instinctively holding his useless sword at the ready; flesh a-crawl, hair a-prickle, yet still a king of kings, as ready to challenge the powers of the unknown dead as the powers of the living.

The phantom came straight on, giving them no heed; Kull shrank back as it passed them, feeling an icy breath like a breeze from the arctic snow. Straight on went the shape with slow, silent footsteps, as if the chains of all the ages were upon those vague feet; vanishing about a bend of the corridor.

"Valka!" muttered the Pict, wiping the cold beads from his brow; "that was no man! That was a ghost!"

"Aye!" Kull shook his head wonderingly. "Did you not recognize the face? That was Eallal, who reigned in Valusia a thousand years ago and who was found hideously murdered in his throneroom—the room now known as the Accursed Room. Have you not seen his statue in the Fame Room of Kings?"

"Yes, I remember the tale now. Gods, Kull! that is another sign of the frightful and foul power of the snake priests—that king was slain by snake-people and thus his soul became their slave, to do their bidding throughout eternity! For the sages have ever maintained that if a man is slain by a snake-man his ghost becomes their slave."

A shudder shook Kull's gigantic frame. "Valka! But what a fate! Hark ye"—his fingers closed upon Brule's sinewy arm like steel—"hark ye! If I am wounded unto death by these foul monsters, swear that ye will smite your sword through my breast lest my soul be enslaved."

"I swear," answered Brule, his fierce eyes lighting. "And do ye the same by me, Kull."

Their strong right hands met in a silent sealing of their bloody bargain.

4. Masks

Kull sat upon his throne and gazed broodily out upon the sea of faces turned toward him. A courtier was speaking in evenly modulated tones, but the king scarcely heard him. Close by, Tu, chief councilor, stood ready at Kull's command, and each time the king looked at him, Kull shuddered inwardly. The surface of court life was as the unrippled surface of the sea between tide and tide. To the musing king the affairs of the night before seemed as a dream, until his eyes dropped to the arm of his throne. A brown, sinewy hand rested there, upon the wrist of which gleamed a dragon armlet; Brule stood beside his throne and ever the Pict's fierce secret whisper brought him back from the realm of unreality in which he moved.

No, that was no dream, that monstrous interlude. As he sat upon his throne in the Hall of Society and gazed upon the courtiers, the ladies, the lords, the statesmen, he seemed to see their faces as things of illusion, things unreal, existent only as shadows and mockeries of substance. Always he had seen their faces as masks, but before he had looked on them with contemptuous tolerance, thinking to see beneath the masks shallow, puny souls, avaricious, lustful, deceitful; now there was a grim undertone, a sinister meaning, a vague horror that lurked beneath the smooth masks. While he exchanged courtesies with some nobleman or councilor he seemed to see the smiling face fade like smoke and the frightful jaws of a serpent gaping there. How many of those he looked upon were horrid, inhuman monsters, plotting his death, beneath the smooth mesmeric illusion of a human face?

Valusia—land of dreams and nightmares—a kingdom of the shadows, ruled by phantoms who glided back and forth behind the painted curtains, mocking the futile king who sat upon the throne—himself a shadow.

And like a comrade shadow Brule stood by his side, dark eyes glittering from immobile face. A real man, Brule! And Kull felt his friendship for the savage become a thing of reality and sensed that Brule felt a friendship for him beyond the mere necessity of statecraft.

And what, mused Kull, were the realities of life? Ambition, power, pride? The friendship of man, the love of women—which Kull had never known—battle, plunder, what? Was it the real Kull who sat upon the throne or was it the real Kull who had scaled the hills of Atlantis, harried the far isles of the sunset, and laughed upon the green roaring tides of the Atlantean sea? How could a man be so many different men in a lifetime? For Kull knew that there were many Kulls and he wondered which was the real Kull. After all, the priests of the Serpent went a step further in their magic, for all men wore masks, and many a different mask with each different man or woman; and Kull wondered if a serpent did not lurk under every mask.

So he sat and brooded in strange, mazy thought ways, and the courtiers came and went and the minor affairs of the day were completed, until at last the king and Brule sat alone in the Hall of Society save for the drowsy attendants.

Kull felt a weariness. Neither he nor Brule had slept the night before, nor had Kull slept the night before that, when in the gardens of Ka-nu he had had his first hint of the weird things to be. Last night nothing further had occurred after they had returned to the study room from the secret corridors, but they had neither dared nor cared to sleep. Kull, with the incredible vitality of a wolf, had aforetime gone for days upon days without sleep, in his wild savage days but now his mind was edged from constant thinking and from the nervebreaking eeriness of the past night. He needed sleep, but sleep was furthest from his mind.

And he would not have dared sleep if he had thought of it. Another thing that had shaken him was the fact that though he and Brule had kept a close watch to see if, or when, the study-room guard was changed, yet it was changed without their knowledge; for the next morning those who stood on guard were able to repeat the magic words of Brule, but they remembered nothing out of the ordinary. They thought that they had stood at guard all night, as usual, and Kull said nothing to the contrary. He believed them true men, but Brule had advised absolute secrecy, and Kull also thought it best.

Now Brule leaned over the throne, lowering his voice so not even a lazy attendant could hear: " They will strike soon, I think, Kull. A while ago Ka-nu gave me a secret sign. The priests know that we know of their plot, of course, but they know not, how much we know. We must be ready for any sort of action. Ka-nu and the Pictish chiefs will remain within hailing distance now until this is settled one way or another. Ha, Kull, if it comes to a pitched battle, the streets and the castles of Valusia will run red!"

Kull smiled grimly. He would greet any sort of action with a ferocious joy. This wandering in a labyrinth of illusion and magic was extremely irksome to his nature. He longed for the leap and clang of swords, for the joyous freedom of battle.

Then into the Hall of Society came Tu again, and the rest of the councilors.

"Lord king, the hour of the council is at hand and we stand ready to escort you to the council room."

Kull rose, and the councilors bent the knee as he passed through the way opened by them for his passage, rising behind him, and following. Eyebrows were raised as the Pict strode defiantly behind the king, but no one dissented. Brule's challenging gaze swept the smooth faces of the councilors with the defiance of an intruding savage.

The group passed through the halls and came at last to the council chamber. The door was closed, as usual, and the councilors arranged themselves in the order of their rank before the dais upon which stood the king. Like a bronze statue Brule took up his stand behind Kull.

Kull swept the room with a swift stare. Surely no chance of treachery here. Seventeen councilors there were, all known to him; all of them had espoused his cause when he ascended the throne.

"Men of Valusia—" he began in the conventional manner, then halted, perplexed. The councilors had risen as a man and were moving toward him. There was no hostility in their looks, but their actions were strange for a council room. The foremost was close to him when Brule sprang forward, crouched like a leopard.

"Ka. nama. kaa. lajerama!" his voice crackled through the sinister silence of the room and the foremost councilor recoiled, hand flashing to his robes; and like a spring released Brule moved and the man pitched headlong to the glint of his sword—headlong he pitched and lay still while his face faded and became the head of a mighty snake.

"Slay, Kull!" rasped the Pict's voice. "They be all serpent men!"

The rest was a scarlet maze. Kull saw the familiar faces dim like fading fog and in their places gaped horrid reptilian visages as the whole band rushed forward. His mind was dazed but his giant body faltered not.

The singing of his sword filled the room, and the onrushing flood broke in a red wave. But they surged forward again, seemingly willing to fling their lives away in order to drag down the king. Hideous jaws gaped at him; terrible eyes blazed into his unblinkingly; a frightful fetid scent pervaded the atmosphere—the serpent scent that Kull had known in southern jungles. Swords and daggers leaped at him and he was dimly aware that they wounded him. But Kull was in his element; never before had he faced such grim foes but it mattered little; they lived, their veins held blood that could be spilt and they died when his great sword cleft their skulls or drove through their bodies. Slash, thrust, thrust and swing. Yet had Kull died there but for the man who crouched at his side, parrying and thrusting. For the king was clear berserk, fighting in the terrible Atlantean way, that seeks death to deal death; he made no effort to avoid thrusts and slashes, standing straight up and ever plunging forward, no thought in his frenzied mind but to slay. Not often did Kull forget his fighting craft in his primitive fury, but now some chain had broken in his soul, flooding his mind with a red wave of slaughter-lust. He slew a foe at each blow, but they surged about him, and time and again Brule turned a thrust that would have slain, as he crouched beside Kull, parrying and warding with cold skill, slaying not as Kull slew with long slashes and plunges, but with short overhand blows and upward thrusts.

Kull laughed, a laugh of insanity. The frightful faces swirled about him in a scarlet blaze. He felt steel sink into his arm and dropped his sword in a flashing arc that cleft his foe to the breast-bone. Then the mists faded and the king saw that he and Brule stood alone above a sprawl of hideous crimson figures who lay still upon the floor.

"Valka! what a killing!" said Brule, shaking the blood from his eyes. "Kull, had these been warriors who knew how to use the steel, we had died here. These serpent priests know naught of swordcraft and die easier than any men I ever slew. Yet had there been a few more, I think the matter had ended otherwise."

Kull nodded. The wild berserker blaze had passed, leaving a mazed feeling of great weariness. Blood seeped from wounds on breast, shoulder, arm and leg. Brule, himself bleeding from a score of flesh wounds, glanced at him in some concern.

"Lord Kull, let us hasten to have your wounds dressed by the women."

Kull thrust him aside with a drunken sweep of his mighty arm.

"Nay, we'll see this through ere we cease. Go you, though, and have your wounds seen to—I command it."

The Pict laughed grimly. "Your wounds are more than mine, lord king—" he began, then stopped as a sudden thought struck him. "By Valka, Kull, this is not the council room!"

Kull looked about and suddenly other fogs seemed to fade. "Nay, this is the room where Eallal died a thousand years ago—since unused and named 'Accursed'."

"Then by the gods, they tricked us after all!" exclaimed Brule in a fury, kicking the corpses at their feet. "They caused us to walk like fools into their ambush! By their magic they changed the appearance of all—"

"Then there is further deviltry afoot," said Kull, "for if there be true men in the councils of Valusia they should be in the real council room now. Come swiftly."

And leaving the room with its ghastly keepers they hastened through halls that seemed deserted until they came to the real council room. Then Kull halted with a ghastly shudder. *From the council room sounded a voice speaking, and the voice was his!*

With a hand that shook he parted the tapestries and gazed into the room. There sat the councilors, counterparts of the men he and Brule had just slain, and upon the dais stood Kull, king of Valusia.

He stepped back, his mind reeling.

"This is insanity!" he whispered. "Am I Kull? Do I stand here or is that Kull yonder in very truth and am I but a shadow, a figment of thought?"

Brule's hand clutching his shoulder, shaking him fiercely, brought him to his senses.

"Valka's name, be not a fool! Can you yet be astounded after all we have seen? See you not that those are true men bewitched by a snake-man who has taken your form, as those others took their forms? By now you should have been slain and yon monster reigning in your stead, unknown by those who bowed to you. Leap and slay swiftly or else we are undone. The Red Slayers, true men, stand close on each hand and none but you can reach and slay him. Be swift!"

Kull shook off the onrushing dizziness, flung back his head in the old, defiant gesture. He took a long, deep breath as does a strong swimmer before diving into the sea; then, sweeping back the tapestries, made the dais in a single lion-like bound. Brule had spoken truly. There stood men of the Red Slayers, guardsmen trained to move quick as the striking leopard; any but Kull had died ere he could reach the usurper. But the sight of Kull, identical with the man upon the dais, held them in their tracks, their minds stunned for an instant, and that was long enough. He upon the dais snatched for his sword, but even as his fingers closed upon the hilt, Kull's sword stood out behind his shoulders and the thing that men had thought the king pitched forward from the dais to lie silent upon the floor.

"Hold!" Kull's lifted hand and kingly voice stopped the rush that had started, and while they stood astounded he pointed to the thing which lay before them—whose face was fading into that of a snake. They recoiled, and from one door came Brule and from another came Ka-nu.

These grasped the king's bloody hand and Ka-nu spoke: "Men of Valusia, you have seen with your own eyes. This is the true Kull, the mightiest king to whom Valusia has ever bowed. The power of the Serpent is broken and ye be all true men. King Kull, have you commands?"

"Lift that carrion," said Kull, and men of the guard took up the thing.

"Now follow me," said the king, and he made his way to the Accursed Room. Brule, with a look of concern, offered the support of his arm but Kull shook him off.

The distance seemed endless to the bleeding king, but at last he stood at the door and laughed fiercely and grimly when he heard the horrified ejaculations of the councilors.

At his orders the guardsmen flung the corpse they carried beside the others, and motioning all from the room Kull stepped out last and closed the door.

A wave of dizziness left him shaken. The faces turned to him, pallid and wonderingly, swirled and mingled in a ghostly fog. He felt the blood from his wound trickling down his limbs and he knew that what he was to do, he must do quickly or not at all.

His sword rasped from its sheath.

"Brule, are you there?"

"Aye!" Brule's face looked at him through the mist, close to his shoulder, but Brule's voice sounded leagues and eons away.

"Remember our vow, Brule. And now, bid them stand back."

His left arm cleared a space as he flung up his sword. Then with all his waning power he drove it through the door into the jamb, driving the great sword to the hilt and sealing the room forever.

Legs braced wide, he swayed drunkenly, facing the horrified councilors. "Let this room be doubly accursed. And let those rotting skeletons lie there forever as a sign of the dying might of the Serpent. Here I swear that I shall hunt the serpent-men from land to land, from sea to sea, giving no rest until all be slain, that good triumph and the power of Hell be broken. This thing I swear— I—Kull—king—of—Valusia."

His knees buckled as the faces swayed and swirled.

The councilors leaped forward, but ere they could reach him, Kull slumped to the floor, and lay still, face upward.

The councilors surged about the fallen king, chattering and shrieking. Ka-nu beat them back with his clenched fists, cursing savagely.

"Back, you fools! Would you stifle the little life that is yet in him? How, Brule, is he dead or will he live?"— to the warrior who bent above the prostrate Kull.

"Dead?" sneered Brule irritably. "Such a man as this is not so easily killed. Lack of sleep and loss of blood have weakened him—by Valka, he has a score of deep wounds, but none of them mortal. Yet have those gibbering fools bring the court women here at once."

Brule's eyes lighted with a fierce, proud light.

"Valka, Ka-nu, but here is such a man as I knew not existed in these degenerate days. He will be in the saddle in a few scant days and then may the serpent-men of the world beware of Kull of Valusia. Valka! but that will be a rare hunt! Ah, I see long years of prosperity for the world with such a king upon the throne of Valusia."

THE ALTAR AND THE SCORPION

"God of the crawling darkness, grant me aid!"

A slim youth knelt in the gloom, his white body shimmering like ivory. The polished marble floor was cold to his knees, but his heart was colder than the stone.

High above him, merged into the masking shadows, loomed the great lapis lazuli ceiling, upheld by marble walls. Before him glimmered a golden altar, and on this altar shone a huge crystal image: a scorpion, wrought with a craft surpassing mere art.

"Great Scorpion," the youth continued his invocation, "aid thy worshipper! Thou knowest how in bygone days Gonra of the Sword, my greatest ancestor, died before thy shrine on a heap of slain barbarians who sought to defile thy holiness. Through the mouths of thy priests, thou promised aid to Gonra's race for all the years to come.

"Great Scorpion! Never has man or woman of my blood before reminded thee of thy vow. But now in my hour of bitter need I come before thee, to abjure thee to remember that oath, by the blood drunk by Gonra's blade, by the blood spilled from Gonra's veins!

"Great Scorpion! Thuron, high priest of The Black Shadow, is my enemy. Kull, king of all Valusia, rides from his purple-spired city to smite with fire and steel the priests who have defied him and still offer human

51

sacrifice to the dark elder gods. But before the king may arrive and save us, I, and the girl I love, shall lie stark on the black altar in the Temple of Everlasting Darkness. Thuron has sworn! He will give our bodies to ancient and abhorred abominations, and, at last, our souls to the god that lurks forever in The Black Shadow.

"Kull sits high on the throne of Valusia and now rides to our aid, but Thuron rules this mountain city and even now follows me. Great Scorpion, aid us! Remember Gonra, who gave up his life for you when the Atlantean savages carried the torch and sword into Valusia."

The boy's slender form drooped, his head sank on his bosom despairingly. The great shimmering image on the altar gave back an icy sheen in the dim light, and no sign came to its worshipper to show that the curious god had heard that passionate invocation.

Suddenly the youth started erect. Quick footfalls throbbed on the long wide steps outside the temple. A girl darted into the shadowed doorway like a white flame blown before the wind.

"Thuron—he comes!" she gasped as she flew into her lover's arms.

The boy's face went pale, and his embrace tightened as he gazed apprehensively at the doorway. Footfalls, heavy and sinister, clashed on the marble, and a shape of menace loomed in the opening.

Thuron, the high priest, was a tall, gaunt man, a cadaverous giant. His eyes glimmered like fiery pools under his heavy brows, and his thin gash of a mouth gaped in a silent laugh. His only garment was a silken loincloth, through which was thrust a cruel curved dagger, and he carried a short, heavy whip in his lean, powerful hand.

His two victims clung to each other and gazed wide-eyed at their foe, as birds stare at a serpent. And Thuron's slow, swaying stride as he advanced was not unlike the sinuous glide of a crawling snake.

"Thuron, have a care!" the youth spoke bravely, but his voice faltered from the terror that gripped him. "If you have no fear of the king or pity for us, beware offending the Great Scorpion, under whose protection we are."

Thuron laughed in his might and arrogance.

"The king!" he jeered. "What means the king to me, who am mightier than any king? The Great Scorpion? Ho! ho! A forgotten god, a deity remembered only by children and women. Would you pit your Scorpion against The Black Shadow? Fool! Valka himself, god of all gods, could not save you now! You are sworn to the god of The Black Shadow."

He swept toward the cowering youngsters and gripped their white shoulders, sinking his talon-like nails deep into the soft flesh. They sought to resist, but he laughed and with incredible strength lifted them in the air, where he dangled them at arms' length as a man might dangle a baby. His grating, metallic laughter filled the room with echoes of evil mockery.

Holding the youth between his knees, he bound the girl hand and foot while she whimpered in his cruel clutch; then, flinging her roughly to the floor, he bound the youth likewise. Stepping back, he surveyed his work. The girl's frightened sobs sounded quick and panting in the silence. At last the high priest spoke.

"Fools, to think to escape me! Always men of your blood, boy, have opposed me in council and court. Now you pay, and The Black Shadow drinks. Ho! ho! I rule the city today, let he be king who may!

"My priests throng the streets, full armed, and no man dare say me nay. Were the king in the saddle this moment, he could not arrive and break my swordsmen in time to save you."

His eyes roved about the temple and fell upon the golden altar and the silent crystal scorpion.

"Ho! ho! What fools to pin your faith on a god whom men have long ceased to worship! Who has not even a priest to attend him, and who is granted a shrine only because of the memory of his former greatness; who is accorded reverence only by simple people and foolish women!

"The real gods are dark and bloody! Remember my words when soon you lie on an ebon altar behind which broods a black shadow forever. Before you die you shall know the real gods, the powerful, the terrible gods, who came from forgotten worlds and lost realms of blackness. Who had their birth on frozen stars, and black suns brooding beyond the light of any stars. You shall know the brain-shattering truth of that Unnamable One, to whose reality no earthly likeness may be given, but whose symbol is—The Black Shadow!"

The girl ceased to cry, frozen, like the youth, into dazed silence. They sensed, behind these threats, a hideous and inhuman gulf of monstrous shadows.

Thuron took a stride toward them, bent and reached claw-like hands to grip and lift them to his shoulders. He laughed as they sought to writhe away from him. His fingers closed on the girl's tender shoulder—

A scream shattered the crystal gong of the silence into a million vibrating shards as Thuron bounded into the air and fell on his face, screeching and writhing. Some small creature scurried away and vanished through the door. Thuron's screams dwindled into a high, thin squealing and broke short at the highest note. Silence fell like a deathly mist.

At last the boy spoke in an awed whisper.

"What was it?"

"A scorpion!" the girl's answer came low and tremulous. "It crawled across my bare bosom without harming me, and when Thuron seized me it stung him."

Another silence fell. Then the boy spoke again, hesitantly.

"No scorpion has been seen in this city for longer than men remember."

"The Great One summoned this of his people to our aid!" whispered the girl. "The gods never forget, and the Great Scorpion has kept his oath. Let us give thanks to him!"

And, bound hand and foot as they were, the youthful lovers wriggled about on their faces, where they lay giving praise to the great silent, glistening scorpion on the altar for a long time—until a distant clash of many silver-shod hoofs and the clangor of swords bore to them the coming of the king.

DELCARDES' CAT

King Kull went with Tu, chief councilor of the throne, to see the talking cat of Delcardes, for though a cat may look at a king, it is not given every king a look at a cat like Delcardes'. So Kull forgot the death threat of Thulsa Doom, the necromancer, and went to Delcardes.

Kull was skeptical, and Tu was wary and suspicious without knowing why, but years of counter-plot and intrigue had soured him. He swore testily that a talking cat was a fraud, a swindle, and a delusion; and maintained that should such a thing exist, it was a direct insult to the gods, who ordained that only man should enjoy the power of speech.

But Kull knew that in the old times beasts had talked to men, for he had heard the legends, handed down from his barbarian ancestors. So he was skeptical but open to conviction.

Delcardes helped the conviction. She lounged with supple ease upon her silk couch, like a great, beautiful feline, and looked at Kull from under long, drooping lashes, which lent unimaginable charm to her narrow, piquantly slanted eyes.

Her lips were full and red, and usually, as at present, curved in a faint enigmatical smile. Her silken garments and ornaments of gold and gems hid little of her glorious figure.

But Kull was not interested in women. He ruled Valusia, but for all that, he was an Atlantean and a savage in the eyes of his subjects. War and conquest held his attention, together with keeping his feet on the ever-rocking throne of the ancient empire, and the task of learning the customs and thoughts of the people he ruled.

To Kull, Delcardes was a mysterious and queenly figure, alluring, yet surrounded by a haze of ancient wisdom and womanly magic.

To Tu, she was a woman and therefore the latent base of intrigue and danger.

To Ka-nu, Pictish ambassador and Kull's closest adviser, she was an eager child, parading under the effect of her play-acting; but Ka-nu was not there when Kull came to see the talking cat.

The cat lolled on a silken cushion on a couch of her own, and surveyed the king with inscrutable eyes. Her name was Saremes, and she had a slave who stood behind her, ready to do her bidding; a lanky man who kept the lower part of his face concealed by a thin veil which fell to his chest.

"King Kull," said Delcardes, "I crave a boon of you before Saremes begins to speak, when I must be silent."

"You may speak," Kull answered.

The girl smiled eagerly and clasped her hands.

"Let me marry Kulra Thoom of Zarfhaana."

Tu broke in as Kull was about to speak.

"My lord, this matter has been thrashed out at lengths before! I thought there was some purpose in requesting this visit! This—this girl has a strain of royal blood in her, and it is against the custom of Valusia that royal women should marry foreigners of lower rank."

"But the king can rule otherwise," pouted Delcardes.

"My lord," said Tu, spreading his hands as one in the last stages of nervous irritation, "if she marries thus it is likely to cause war and rebellion and discord for the next hundred years."

He was about to plunge into a dissertation on rank, genealogy, and history; but Kull interrupted, his short stock of patience exhausted.

"Valka and Hotath! Am I an old woman or a priest to be bedeviled with such affairs? Settle it between yourselves and vex me no more with questions of mating! By Valka, in Atlantis men and women marry whom they please and none else."

Delcardes pouted a little, made a face at Tu, who scowled back; then smiled sunnily and turned on her couch with a lissome movement.

"Talk to Saremes, Kull; she will grow jealous of me."

Kull eyed the cat uncertainly. Her fur was long, silky, and gray; her eyes slanting and mysterious.

"She looks very young, Kull; yet she is very old," said Delcardes. "She is a cat of the Old Race who lived to be thousands of years old. Ask her age, Kull."

"How many years have you seen, Saremes?" asked Kull idly.

"Valusia was young when I was old," the cat answered in a clear though curiously timbered voice.

Kull started violently.

"Valka and Hotath!" he swore. "She talks!"

Delcardes laughed softly in pure enjoyment, but the expression of the cat never altered.

"I talk, I think, I know, I *am*," she said. "I have been the ally of queens and the councilor of kings ages before the white beaches of Atlantis knew your feet, Kull of Valusia. I saw the ancestors of the Valusians ride out of the far east to trample down the Old Race, and I was here when the Old Race came up out of the oceans so many eons ago that the mind of man reels when seeking to measure them. Older am I than Thulsa Doom, whom few men have ever seen. I have seen empires rise and kingdoms fall and kings ride in on their steeds and out on their shields. Aye, I have been a goddess in my time, and strange were the neophytes who bowed before me and terrible were the rites which were performed in my worship. For of old, beings exalted my kind—beings as strange as their deeds."

"Can you read the stars and foretell events?" Kull's barbarian mind at once leaped to material ideas.

"Aye, the books of the past and the future are open to me, and I tell man what is good for him to know."

"Then tell me," said Kull, "where I misplaced the secret letter from Ka-nu yesterday."

"You thrust it into the bottom of your dagger scabbard and then instantly forgot it," the cat replied.

Kull started, snatched out his dagger, and shook the sheath. A thin strip of folded parchment tumbled out.

"Valka and Hotath!" he swore. "Saremes, you are a witch of cats! Mark ye, Tu!"

But Tu's lips were pressed in a straight, disapproving line, and he eyed Delcardes darkly.

She returned his stare guilelessly, and he turned to Kull in irritation.

"My lord, consider! This is all mummery of some sort."

"Tu, none saw me hide that letter, for I myself had forgotten."

"Lord king, any spy might—"

"Spy? Be not a greater fool than you were born, Tu. Shall a cat set spies to watch me hide letters?"

Tu sighed. As he grew older it was becoming increasingly difficult to refrain from showing exasperation toward kings.

"My lord, give thought to the humans who may be behind the cat!"

"Lord Tu," said Delcardes in a tone of gentle reproach, "you put me to shame, and you offend Saremes."

Kull felt vaguely angered at Tu.

"At least, Tu," said he, "the cat talks; that you cannot deny."

"There is some trickery," Tu stubbornly maintained. "Man talks; beasts may not."

"Not so," said Kull, himself convinced of the reality of

the talking cat, and anxious to prove that he was correct. "A lion talked to Kambra, and birds have spoken to the old men of the Sea-mountain tribe, telling them where game was hidden.

"None denies that beasts talk among themselves. Many a night have I lain on the slopes of the forest-covered hills or out on the grassy savannahs, and have heard the tigers roaring to one another across the starlight. Then why should some beast not learn the speech of man? There have been times when I could almost understand the roaring of the tigers. The tiger is my totem and is tabu to me, save in self-defense," he added irrelevantly.

Tu squirmed. This talk of totem and tabu was good enough in a savage chief, but to hear such remarks from the king of Valusia irked him extremely.

"My lord," said he, "a cat is not a tiger."

"Very true," said Kull. "And this one is wiser than all tigers."

"That is naught but truth," said Saremes calmly.

"Lord chancellor, would you believe then if I told you what was at this moment transpiring at the royal treasury?"

"No!" Tu snarled. "Clever spies may learn anything, as I have found."

"No man can be convinced when he will not," said Saremes imperturbably, quoting an ancient Valusian saying. "Yet know, lord Tu, that a surplus of twenty gold tals has been discovered, and a courier is even now hastening through the streets to tell you of it. Ah," as a step sounded in the corridor without, "even now he comes."

A slim courtier, clad in the gay garments of the royal treasury, entered, bowing deeply, and craved permission to speak. Kull having granted it, he said:

"Mighty king and lord Tu, a surplus of twenty tals of gold has been found in the royal moneys."

Delcardes laughed and clapped her hands delightedly, but Tu merely scowled.

"When was this discovered?"

"A scant half-hour ago."

"How many have been told of it?"

"None, my lord. Only I and the royal treasurer have known until just now when I told you, my lord."

"Humph!" Tu waved him aside sourly. "Begone. I will see about this matter later."

"Delcardes," said Kull, "this cat is yours, is she not?"

"Lord king," answered the girl, "no one owns Saremes. She only bestows on me the honor of her presence; she is a guest. She is her own mistress and has been for a thousand years."

"I would that I might keep her in the palace," said Kull.

"Saremes," said Delcardes deferentially, "the king would have you as his guest."

"I will go with the king of Valusia," said the cat with dignity, "and remain in the royal palace until such time as it shall pleasure me to go elsewhere. For I am a great traveler, Kull, and it pleases me at times to go out over the world and walk the streets of cities where in ages gone by I have roamed forests, and to tread the sands of deserts where long ago I trod imperial streets."

So Saremes, the talking cat, came to the royal palace of Valusia. Her slave accompanied her, and she was given a spacious chamber lined with fine couches and silken pillows. The best viands of the royal table were placed before her daily, and all the household of the king did homage to her except Tu, who grumbled to see a cat exalted, even a talking cat. Saremes treated him with amused contempt, but admitted Kull into a level of dignified equality.

She quite often came into his throne chamber, borne on a silken cushion by her slave, who must always accompany her, no matter where she went.

At other times Kull came into her chamber, and they talked into the dim hours of dawn, and many were the tales she told him and ancient the wisdom that she imparted. Kull listened with interest and attention, for it was evident that this cat was wiser far than many of his councilors, and had gained more ancient wisdom than all of them together. Her words were pithy and oracular, but she refused to prophesy beyond minor affairs taking place in the everyday life of the palace or kingdom; save that she warned him against Thulsa Doom, who had sent a threat to Kull.

"For," said she, "I, who have lived more years than you shall live minutes, know that man is better off without knowledge of things to come; for what is to be, will be, and man can neither avert nor hasten. It is better to go in the dark when the road must pass a lion and there is no other road."

"Yes," said Kull, "if what must be, is to be—a thing which I doubt—and a man be told what things shall come to pass and his arm weakened or strengthened thereby; then was that, too, foreordained?"

"If he was ordained to be told," said Saremes, adding to Kull's perplexity and doubt. "However, not all of life's roads are set fast, for a man may do this or a man may do that, and not even the gods know the mind of a man."

"Then," said Kull dubiously, "all things are not destined if there be more than one road for a man to follow. And how can events then be prophesied truly?"

"Life has many roads, Kull," answered Saremes. "I stand at the crossroads of the world, and I know what lies down each road. Still, not even the gods know what road a man will take, whether the right hand or the left hand, when he comes to the dividing of the ways; and once started upon a road, he cannot retrace his steps."

"Then, in Valka's name," said Kull, "why not point out to me the perils or the advantages of each road as it comes and aid me in choosing?"

"Because there are bounds set upon the powers of such as I," the cat replied, "lest we hinder the workings of the alchemy of the gods. We may not brush the veil entirely aside for human eyes, lest the gods take our power from us, and lest we do harm to man. For though there are many roads at each crossroads, still a man must take one of those and sometimes one is no better than another. So Hope flickers her lamp along one road and man follows, though that road may be the foulest of all."

Then she continued, seeing Kull found it difficult to understand.

"You see, lord king, that our powers must have limits, else we might grow too powerful and threaten the gods. So a mystic spell is laid upon us, and while we may open the books of the past, we may but grant flying glances of the future through the mist that veils it."

Kull felt somehow that the argument of Saremes was rather flimsy and illogical, smacking of witchcraft and mummery; but with Saremes' cold, oblique eyes gazing unwinkingly at him, he was not prone to offer any objections, even had he thought of any.

"Now," said the cat, "I will draw aside the veil for an instant to your own good—let Delcardes marry Kulra Thoom."

Kull rose with an impatient twitch of his mighty shoulders.

"I will have naught to do with a woman's mating. Let Tu attend to it."

Yet Kull slept on the thought, and as Saremes wove the advice craftily into her philosophizing and moralizing in days to come, Kull weakened.

A strange sight it was indeed, to see Kull, his chin resting on his great fist, leaning forward and drinking in the distinct intonations of the cat Saremes as she lay curled on her silken cushion, or stretched languidly at full length; as she talked of mysterious and fascinating subjects, her eyes glinting strangely and her lips scarcely moving, if at all, while the slave Kuthulos stood behind her like a statue, motionless and speechless.

Kull highly valued her opinions, and he was prone to ask her advice—which she gave warily or not at all—on matters of state. Still, Kull found that what she advised usually coincided with his private wish, and he began to wonder if she were not a mind reader also.

Kuthulos irked him with his gauntness, his motionlessness, and his silence, but Saremes would have none other to attend her. Kull strove to pierce the veil that masked the man's features, but though it seemed thin enough, he could tell nothing of the face beneath and out of courtesy to Saremes never asked Kuthulos to unveil.

Kull came to the chamber of Saremes one day, and she looked at him with enigmatical eyes. The masked slave stood statue-like behind her.

"Kull," said she, "again I will tear the veil for you. Brule, the Pictish Spear-slayer, warrior of Ka-nu and your friend, has just been hauled beneath the surface of the Forbidden Lake by a grisly monster."

Kull sprang up, cursing in rage and alarm.

"Ha! Brule? Valka's name, what was he doing about the Forbidden Lake?"

"He was swimming there. Hasten, you may yet save him, even though he be borne to the Enchanted Land which lies below the Lake."

Kull whirled toward the door. He was startled, but not so much as he would have been had the swimmer been someone else, for he knew the reckless irreverence of the Pict, chief among Valusia's most powerful allies.

He started to shout for guards, when Saremes' voice stayed him.

"Nay, my lord. You had best go alone. Not even your command might make men accompany you into the waters of that grim lake, and by the custom of Valusia, it is death for any man to enter there save the king."

"Aye, I will go alone," said Kull, "and thus save Brule from the anger of the people, should he chance to escape the monsters. Inform Ka-nu."

Kull, discouraging respectful inquiries with wordless snarls, mounted his great stallion and rode out of Valusia at full speed. He rode alone and he ordered that none follow him. That which he had to do, he could do alone, and he did not wish anyone to see when he brought Brule or Brule's corpse out of the Forbidden Lake. He cursed the reckless inconsideration of the Pict, and he cursed the tabu which hung over the lake; the violation of which might cause rebellion among the Valusians.

Twilight was stealing down from the mountains of Zalgara when Kull halted his horse on the shores of the lake, which lay amid a great lonely forest. There was certainly nothing forbidding in its appearance, for its waters spread blue and placid from beach to wide white beach, and the tiny islands rising about its bosom seemed like gems of emerald and jade. A faint shimmering mist rose from it, enhancing the air of lazy unreality which lay about the regions of the lake. Kull listened intently for a moment, and it seemed to him as though faint and faraway music breathed up through the sapphire waters.

He cursed impatiently, wondering if he were beginning to be bewitched, and flung aside all garments and ornaments except his girdle, loin-clout, and sword. He waded out into the shimmery blueness until it lapped his thighs; then, knowing that the depth swiftly increased, he drew a deep breath and dived.

As he swam down through the sapphire glimmer, he had time to reflect that this was probably a fool's errand. He might have taken time to find from Saremes just where Brule had been swimming when attacked and whether he was destined to rescue the warrior or not. Still, he thought that the cat might not have told him, and even if she had assured him of failure, he would have attempted what he was now doing, anyway. So there was truth in Saremes' saying that men were better untold about the future.

As for the location of the site where Brule had been attacked, the monster might have dragged him anywhere. Kull intended to explore the lake bed until—

Even as he ruminated thus, a shadow flashed by him, a vague shimmer in the jade and sapphire shimmer of the lake. He was aware that other shadows swept by him on all sides, but he could not make out their forms.

Far beneath him he began to see the glimmer of the lake bottom which seemed to glow with a strange radiance. Now the shadows were all about him; they wove a serpentine net about him, an ever-changing thousand-hued glittering web of color. The water here burned topaz and the things wavered and scintillated in its faery splendor. Like the shades and shadows of colors they were, vague and unreal, yet opaque and gleaming.

However, Kull, deciding that they had no intention of attacking him, gave them no more attention, but directed his gaze on the lake floor which his feet just then lightly struck. He started, and could have sworn that he had landed on a living creature, for he felt rhythmic movement beneath his bare feet. The faint glow was evident there at the bottom of the lake; as far as he could see, stretching away on all sides until it faded into the lambent sapphire shadows, the lake floor was one solid level of fire that faded and glowed with unceasing regularity. Kull bent closer; the floor was covered by a sort of short moss-like substance which shone like white flame. It was as if the lake bed were covered with myriads of fireflies which raised and lowered their wings together. And this moss throbbed beneath his feet like a living thing.

Now Kull began to swim upward again. Raised among the sea-mountains of ocean-girt Atlantis, he was like a sea creature himself. As much at home in the water as any Lemurian, he could remain under the surface twice as long as the ordinary swimmer, but this lake was deep and he wished to conserve his strength.

He came to the top, filled his enormous chest with air, and dived again. Again the shadows swept about him, almost dazzling his eyes with their ghostly gleams. He swam faster this time, and having reached the bottom, he began to walk along it as fast as the clinging substance about his limbs would allow; the while the fire-moss breathed and glowed and the color things flashed about him and monstrous, nightmarish shadows fell across his shoulder upon the burning floor, flung by unseen beings.

The moss was littered by the skulls and the bones of men who had dared the Forbidden Lake. Suddenly, with a silent swirl of the waters, a thing rushed upon Kull. At first the king thought it to be a huge octopus, for the body was that of an octopus, with long waving tentacles; but as it charged upon him he saw that it had legs like a man and a hideous semi-human face leered at him from among the writhing, snaky arms of the monster.

Kull braced his feet, and as he felt the cruel tentacles whip about his limbs, he thrust his sword with cool accuracy into the midst of that demoniac face, and the creature lumbered down and died at his feet with grisly, soundless gibbering. Blood spread like a mist about him, and Kull thrust strongly against the floor with his legs and shot upward.

He burst into the fast-fading light, and even as he did, a great form came skimming across the water toward him—a water spider, but this one was larger than a boar, and its cold eyes gleamed hellishly. Kull, keeping himself afloat with his feet and one hand, raised his sword, and as the spider rushed in, he cleft it halfway through the body; and it sank silently.

A slight noise made him turn, and another, larger than the first, was almost upon him. This one flung over the king's arms and shoulders strands of clinging web that would have meant doom for any but a giant. But Kull burst the grim shackles as if they had been strings, and seizing a leg of the thing as it towered above him, he thrust the monster through again and again till it weakened in his grasp and floated away, reddening the waters.

"Valka!" muttered the king, "I am not like to go without employment here. Yet these things be easy to slay. How could they have overcome Brule, who is second only to me in battle might in all the Seven Kingdoms?"

But Kull was to find that grimmer spectres than these haunted the death-ridden abysses of Forbidden Lake.

Again he dived and this time only the color shadows and the bones of forgotten men met his glance. Again he rose for air and for the fourth time he dived.

He was not far from one of the islands, and as he swam downward, he wondered what strange things were hidden by the dense emerald foliage which cloaked these islands. Legend said that temples and shrines reared there that were never built by human hands, and that on certain nights the lake beings came out of the deeps to enact eery rites there.

The rush came just as his feet struck the moss. It came from behind, and Kull, warned by some primal instinct, whirled just in time to see a great form loom over him— a form neither man nor beast, but horribly compounded of both—to feel gigantic fingers close on arm and shoulder.

He struggled savagely, but the thing held his sword arm helpless, and its talons sank deeply into his left forearm. With a volcanic wrench he twisted about so that he could at least see his attacker. The thing was something like a monstrous shark, but a long, cruel horn, curved like a saber, jutted up from its snout. It had four arms, human in shape but inhuman in size and strength and in the crooked talons of the fingers.

With two arms the monster held Kull helpless, and with the other two it bent his head back to break his spine. But not even such a grim being as this might so easily conquer Kull of Atlantis. A wild rage surged up in him, and the king of Valusia went berserk.

Bracing his feet against the yielding moss, he tore his left arm free with a heave and wrench of his shoulders. With cat-like speed, he sought to shift the sword from right hand to left and, failing in this, struck savagely at the monster with clenched fist. But the mocking sapphirean stuff about him foiled him, breaking the force of his blow. The shark-man lowered his snout, but, before he could strike upward, Kull gripped the horn with his left hand and held fast.

Then followed a test of might and endurance. Kull, unable to move with any speed in the water, knew his only hope was to keep in close and wrestle with his foe in such a manner as to counterbalance the monster's quickness. He strove desperately to tear his sword arm loose, and the shark-man was forced to grasp it with all four of his hands. Kull gripped the horn and dared not let go lest he be disemboweled with its terrible upward thrust, and the shark-man dared not release with a single hand the arm that held Kull's long sword.

So they wrenched and wrestled, and Kull saw that he was doomed if it went on in this manner. Already he was beginning to suffer for want of air. The gleam in the cold eyes of the shark-man told that he, too, recognized the fact that he had but to hold Kull below the surface until he drowned.

A desperate plight indeed, for any man. But Kull of Atlantis was no ordinary man. Trained from childhood in a hard and bloody school, with steel muscles and dauntless brain bound together by the coordination that makes the super-fighter, he added to this a courage which never faltered and a tigerish rage which on occasion swept him up to superhuman deeds.

So now, conscious of his swiftly approaching doom and goaded to frenzy by his helplessness, he decided upon action as desperate as his need. He released the monster's horn, at the same time bending his body as far back as he could and gripping the nearest arm of the thing with the free hand.

Instantly the shark-man struck, his horn ploughing along Kull's thigh and then—the luck of Atlantis!—wedging fast in Kull's heavy girdle. And as he tore it free, Kull sent his mighty strength through the fingers that held the monster's arm, and crushed clammy flesh and inhuman bone like rotten fruit between them.

The shark-man's mouth gaped silently with the torment and he struck again wildly. Kull avoided the blow, and losing their balance, they went down together, half buoyed by the jade surge in which they wallowed. And as they tossed there, Kull tore his sword arm from the weakening grip and, striking upward, split the monster open.

The entire battle had consumed only a very brief time, but to Kull, as he swam upward, his head singing and a great weight seeming to press his ribs, it seemed like hours. He saw dimly that the lake floor shelved suddenly upward close at hand and knew that it sloped to an island; then the water came alive about him and he felt himself lapped from shoulder to heel in gigantic coils which even his steel muscles could not break. His consciousness was fading—he felt himself borne along at terrific speed—there was a sound of many bells—then suddenly he was above water and his tortured lungs were drinking in great draughts of air. He was whirling along through utter darkness, and he had time to take only a long breath before he was again swept under.

Again light glowed about him, and he saw the fire-moss throbbing far below. He was in the grasp of a great serpent who had flung a few lengths of its sinuous body about him like huge cables and was now bearing him to what destination Valka alone knew.

Kull did not struggle, reserving his strength. If the snake did not keep him so long under water that he died, there would no doubt be a chance of battle in the creature's lair or wherever he was being taken. As it was, Kull's limbs were pinioned so close that he could no more free an arm than he could have flown.

The serpent, racing through the blue deeps so swiftly, was the largest Kull had ever seen—a good two hundred feet of jade and golden scales, vividly and wonderfully colored. Its eyes, when they turned toward Kull, were like icy fire, if such a thing can be. Even then Kull's imaginative soul was struck with the bizarreness of the scene: that great green and gold form flying through the burning topaz of the lake, while the shadow-colors weaved dazzlingly about it.

The fire-gemmed floor sloped upward again—either for an island or the lake shore—and a great cavern suddenly appeared before them. The snake glided into this, the fire-moss ceased, and Kull found himself partly above the surface in unlighted darkness. He was borne along in this manner for what seemed like a very long time; then the monster dived again.

Again they came up into light, but such light as Kull had never before seen. A luminous glow shimmered duskily over the face of the waters which lay dark and still. And Kull knew that he was in the Enchanted Domain under the bottom of Forbidden Lake, for this was no earthly radiance; it was a black light, blacker than any darkness; yet it lit the unholy waters so that he could see the dusky glimmer of them and his own dark reflection in them. The coils suddenly loosed from his limbs, and he struck out for a vast bulk that loomed in the shadows in front of him.

Swimming strongly, he approached and saw that it was a great city. On a great level of black stone, it towered up and up until its sombre spires were lost in the blackness above the unhallowed light, which, black also, was yet of a different hue. Huge square-built massive buildings of mighty basaltic-like blocks fronted him as he clambered out of the clammy waters and strode up the steps which were cut into the stone like steps in a wharf. Columns rose gigantically between the buildings.

No gleam of earthly light lessened the grimness of this inhuman city, but from its walls and towers the black light flowed out over the waters in vast throbbing waves.

Kull was aware that in a wide space before him, where the buildings swept away on each side, a huge concourse of beings confronted him. He blinked, striving to accustom his eyes to the strange illumination. The beings came closer, and a whisper ran among them like the waving of grass in the night wind. They were light and shadowy, glimmering against the blackness of their city, and their eyes were eery and luminous.

Then the king saw that one of their number stood in front of the rest. This one was much like a man, and his bearded face was high and noble, but a frown hovered over his magnificent brows.

"You come like a herald of all your race," said this lake-man suddenly. "Bloody and bearing a red sword."

Kull laughed angrily, for this smacked of injustice.

"Valka and Hotath!" said the king. "Most of this blood is mine own and was let by things of your cursed lake."

"Death and ruin follow the course of your race," said the lake-man sombrely. "Do we not know? Aye, we reigned in the lake of blue waters before mankind was even a dream of the gods."

"None molests you—" began Kull.

"They fear to. In the old days men of the earth sought to invade our dark kingdom. And we slew them, and there was war between the sons of man and the people of the lakes. And we came forth and spread terror among the earthlings, for we knew that they bore only death for us and that they yielded only to slaying. And we wove spells and charms and burst their brains and shattered their souls with our magic so they begged for peace, and it was so. The men of earth laid a tabu on this lake so that no man may come here save the king of Valusia. That was thousands of years ago. No man has ever come into the Enchanted Land and gone forth, save as a corpse floating up through the still waters of the upper lake. King of Valusia, or whoever you be, you are doomed."

Kull snarled in defiance.

"I sought not your cursed kingdom. I seek Brule the Spear-slayer whom you dragged down."

"You lie," the lake-man answered. "No man has dared this lake for over a hundred years. You come seeking treasure or to ravish and slay like all your bloody-handed kind. You die!"

And Kull felt the whisperings of magic charms about him; they filled the air and took physical form, floating in the shimmering light like wispy spiderwebs, clutching at him with vague tentacles. But Kull swore impatiently and swept them aside and out of existence with his bare hand. For against the fierce elemental logic of the savage, the magic of decadency had no force.

"You are young and strong," said the lake-king. "The rot of civilization has not yet entered your soul and our charms may not harm you, because you do not understand them. Then we must try other things."

And the lake-beings about him drew daggers and moved upon Kull. Then the king laughed and set his back against a column, gripping his sword hilt until the muscles stood out on his right arm in great ridges.

"This is a game I understand, ghosts," he laughed.

They halted.

"Seek not to evade your doom," said the king of the lake, "for we are immortal and may not be slain by mortal arms."

"You lie, now," answered Kull, with the craft of the barbarian, "for by your own words you feared the death my kind brought among you. You may live forever, but steel can slay you. Take thought among yourselves. You are soft and weak and unskilled in arms; you bear your blades unfamiliarly. I was born and bred to slaying. You will slay me, for there are thousands of you and I but one; yet your charms have failed, and many of you shall die before I fall. I will slaughter you by the scores. Take thought, men of the lake; is my slaying worth the lives it will cost you?"

For Kull knew that beings who slay by steel may be slain by steel, and he was unafraid. A figure of threat and doom, bloody and terrible he loomed above them.

"Aye, consider," he repeated, "is it better that you should bring Brule to me and let us go, or that my corpse shall lie amid sword-torn heaps of your dead when the battle shout is silent? Nay, there be Picts and Lemurians among my mercenaries who will follow my trail even into the Forbidden Lake and will drench the Enchanted Land with your gore if I die here. For they have their own tabus, and they reck not the tabus of the civilized races; nor care they what may happen to Valusia, but think only of me who am of barbarian blood like themselves."

"The old world reels down the road to ruin and forgetfulness," brooded the lake-king. "And we that were all-powerful in bygone days must brook to be bearded in our own kingdom by an arrogant savage. Swear that you will never set foot in Forbidden Lake again and that you will never let the tabus be broken by others, and you shall go free."

"First bring the Spear-slayer to me."

"No such man has ever come to this lake."

"Nay? The cat Saremes told me—"

"Saremes? Aye, we knew her of old when she came swimming down through the green waters and abode for some centuries in the courts of the Enchanted Land; the wisdom of the ages is hers, but I knew not that she spoke the speech of earthly men. Still, there is no such man here, and I swear—"

"Swear not by gods or devils," Kull broke in. "Give your word as a true man."

"I give it," said the lake-king, and Kull believed, for there was a majestic bearing about the king which made Kull feel strangely small and rude.

"And I," said Kull, "give you my word—which has never been broken—that no man shall break the tabu or molest you in any way again."

"And I believe you, for you are different from any earthly man I ever knew. You are a real king and, what is greater, a true man."

Kull thanked him and sheathed his sword, turning toward the steps.

"Know ye how to gain the outer world, king of Valusia?"

"As to that," answered Kull, "if I swim long enough I suppose I shall find the way. I know that the serpent brought me clear through at least one island and possibly many, and that we swam in a cave for a long time."

"You are bold," said the lake-king, "but you might swim forever in the dark."

He raised his hands, and a behemoth swam to the foot of the steps.

"A grim steed," said the lake-king, "but he will bear you safely to the very shore of the upper lake."

"A moment," said Kull. "Am I at present beneath an island, or the mainland—or is this land in truth beneath the lake floor?"

"You are at the centre of the universe as you are always. Time, place, and space are illusions, having no existence save in the mind of man which must set limits and bounds in order to understand. There is only the underlying reality, of which all appearances are but outward manifestations, just as the upper lake is fed by the waters of this real one. Go now, king, for you are a true man even though you be the first wave of the rising tide of savagery which shall overwhelm the world ere it recedes."

Kull listened respectfully, understanding little but realizing that this was high magic. He struck hands with the lake-king, shuddering a little at the feel of that which was flesh, but not human flesh; then he looked once more at the great black buildings rearing silently and the murmuring moth-like forms among them, and he looked out over the shiny jet surface of the waters with the waves of black light crawling like spiders across it. And he turned and went down the stair of the water's edge and sprang on the back of the behemoth.

Eons followed, of dark caves and rushing waters and the whisper of gigantic unseen monsters; sometimes above and sometimes below the surface the behemoth bore the king, and finally the fire-moss leaped up and they swept up through the blue of the burning water; and Kull waded to land.

Kull's stallion stood patiently where the king had left him. The moon was just rising over the lake, whereat Kull swore amazedly.

"A scant hour ago, by Valka, I dismounted here! I had thought that many hours and possibly days had passed since then."

He mounted and rode toward the city of Valusia, reflecting that there might have been some meaning in the lake-king's remarks about the illusion of time.

Kull was weary, angry, and bewildered. The journey through the lake had cleansed him of the blood, but the motion of riding started the gash in his thigh to bleeding again; moreover, the leg was stiff and irked him somewhat. Still, the main thought that presented itself was that Saremes had lied to him, either through ignorance or through malicious forethought, and had come near to sending him to his death. For what reason?

Kull cursed, reflecting what Tu would say. Still, even a talking cat might be innocently wrong, but hereafter Kull determined to lay no weight to the words of such.

Kull rode into the silent silvery streets of the ancient city, and the guards at the gate gaped at his appearance, but wisely refrained from questioning.

He found the palace in an uproar. Swearing, he stalked to his council chamber and thence to the chamber of the cat Saremes. The cat was there, curled imperturbably on her cushion; and grouped about the chamber, each striving to talk down the others, were Tu and the chief councilors. The slave Kuthulos was nowhere to be seen.

Kull was greeted by a wild acclamation of shouts and questions, but he strode straight to Saremes' cushion and glared at her.

"Saremes," said the king, "you lied to me."

The cat stared at him coldly, yawned, and made no reply. Kull stood nonplussed, and Tu seized his arm.

"Kull, where in Valka's name have you been? Whence this blood?"

Kull jerked loose irritably.

"Leave be," he snarled. "This cat sent me on a fool's errand—where is Brule?"

"Kull!"

The king whirled and saw Brule stride through the door, his scanty garments stained by the dust of hard riding. The bronze features of the Pict were immobile, but his dark eyes gleamed with relief.

"Name of seven devils!" said the warrior testily, to hide his emotion. "My riders have combed the hills and the forest for you. Where have you been?"

"Searching the waters of Forbidden Lake for your worthless carcass," answered Kull, with grim enjoyment at the Pict's perturbation.

"Forbidden Lake!" Brule exclaimed with the freedom of the savage. "Are you in your dotage? What would I be doing there? I accompanied Ka-nu yesterday to the Zarfhaanian border and returned to hear Tu ordering out all the army to search for you. My men have since then ridden in every direction except the Forbidden Lake, where we never thought of going."

"Saremes lied to me—" Kull began.

But he was drowned out by a chatter of scolding voices, the main theme being that a king should never ride off so unceremoniously, leaving the kingdom to take care of itself.

"Silence!" roared Kull, lifting his arms, his eyes blazing dangerously. "Valka and Hotath! Am I an urchin to be rated for truancy? Tu, tell me what has occurred."

In the sudden silence which followed his royal outburst, Tu began:

"My lord, we have been duped from the beginning. This cat is, as I have maintained, a delusion and a dangerous fraud."

"Yet—"

"My lord, have you never heard of men who could hurl their voices to a distance, making it appear that another spoke out, or that invisible voices sounded?"

Kull flushed. "Aye, by Valka! Fool that I should have forgotten! An old wizard of Lemuria had that gift. Yet who spoke—"

"Kuthulos!" exclaimed Tu. "Fool am I not to have remembered Kuthulos, a slave, aye, but the greatest scholar and the wisest man in all the Seven Empires. Slave of that she-fiend Delcardes who even now writhes on the rack!"

Kull gave a sharp exclamation.

"Aye," said Tu grimly. "When I entered and found that you had ridden away, none knew where, I suspected treachery, and I sat down and thought hard. And I remembered Kuthulos and his art of voice-throwing and of how the false cat had told you small things but never great prophecies, giving false arguments for reason of refraining.

"So I knew that Delcardes had sent you this cat and Kuthulos to befool you and gain your confidence, and finally send you to your doom. So I sent for Delcardes and ordered her put to the torture so that she might confess all. She planned cunningly. Aye, Saremes must have her slave Kuthulos with her all the time—while he talked through her mouth and put strange ideas in your mind."

"Then where is Kuthulos?" asked Kull.

"He had disappeared when I came to Saremes' chamber, and—"

"Ho, Kull!" a cheery voice boomed from the door and a bearded, elfish figure strode in, accompanied by a slim, frightened girlish shape.

"Ka-nu! Delcardes! So they did not torture you after all!"

"Oh, my lord!" she ran to him and fell on her knees before him, clasping his feet. "Oh, Kull," she wailed, "they accuse me of terrible things! I am guilty of deceiving you, my lord, but I meant no harm! I only wished to marry Kulra Thoom!"

Kull raised her to her feet, perplexed, but pitying her for her evident terror and remorse.

"Kull," said Ka-nu, "it is a good thing I returned when

I did, else you and Tu had tossed the kingdom into the sea!"

Tu snarled wordlessly, always jealous of the Pictish ambassador, who was also Kull's adviser.

"I returned to find the whole palace in an uproar, men rushing hither and yon and falling over one another in doing nothing. I sent Brule and his riders to look for you, and going to the torture chamber—naturally I went first to the torture chamber, since Tu was in charge—"

The chancellor winced.

"Going to the torture chamber," Ka-nu continued placidly, "I found them about to torture little Delcardes, who wept and told all she had to tell, but they did not believe her. She is only an inquisitive child, Kull, in spite of her beauty and all. So I brought her here.

"Now, Kull, Delcardes spoke truth when she said Saremes was her guest and that the cat was very ancient. True; she is a cat of the Old Race and wiser than other cats, going and coming as she pleases—but still a cat. Delcardes had spies in the palace to report to her such small things as the secret letter which you hid in your dagger sheath and the surplus in the treasury—the courtier who reported that was one of her spies and had discovered the surplus and told her before the royal treasurer knew. Her spies were your most loyal retainers; the things they told her harmed you not and aided her, whom they all love, for they knew she meant no harm.

"Her idea was to have Kuthulos, speaking through the mouth of Saremes, gain your confidence through small prophecies and facts which anyone might know, such as warning you against Thulsa Doom. Then, by constantly urging you to let Kulra Thoom marry Delcardes, to accomplish what was Delcardes' only desire."

"Then Kuthulos turned traitor," said Tu.

And at that moment there was a noise at the chamber door, and guards entered, haling between them a tall, gaunt form, his face masked by a veil, his arms bound.

"Kuthulos!"

"Aye, Kuthulos," said Ka-nu, but he seemed not at ease, and his eyes roved restlessly. "Kuthulos, no doubt, with his veil over his face to hide the workings of his mouth and neck muscles as he talked through Saremes."

Kull eyed the silent figure which stood there like a statue. A silence fell over the group, as if a cold wind had passed over them. There was a tenseness in the atmosphere. Delcardes looked at the silent figure and her eyes widened as the guards told in terse sentences how the slave had been captured while trying to escape from the palace down a little used corridor.

Then a tense silence fell again as Kull stepped forward and reached forth a hand to tear the veil from the hidden face. Through the thin fabric Kull felt two eyes burn into his consciousness. None noticed Ka-nu clench his hands and tense himself as if for a terrific struggle.

Then as Kull's hand almost touched the veil, a sudden sound broke the breathless silence—such a sound as a man might make by striking the floor with his forehead or elbow. The noise seemed to come from a wall, and Kull, crossing the room with a stride, smote against a panel from behind which the rapping sounded. A hidden door swung inward, revealing a dusty corridor, upon which lay the bound and gagged form of a man.

They dragged him forth and, standing him upright, unbound him.

"Kuthulos!" shrieked Delcardes.

Kull stared. The man's face, now revealed, was thin and kindly like a teacher of philosophy and morals.

"Yes, my lords and lady," he said. "That man who wears my veil stole upon me through the secret door, struck me down, and bound me. I lay there, hearing him send the king to what he thought was Kull's death, but could do nothing."

"Then who is he?" All eyes turned towards the veiled figure, and Kull stepped forward.

"Lord king, beware!" exclaimed the real Kuthulos. "He—"

Kull tore the veil away with one motion and recoiled with a gasp. Delcardes screamed and her knees gave way; the councilors pressed backwards, faces white, and the guards released their grasp and shrank away, horror-struck.

The face of the man was a bare white skull, in whose eye sockets flamed livid fire!

"Thulsa Doom! Aye, I guessed as much!" exclaimed Ka-nu.

"Aye, Thulsa Doom, fools," the voice echoed cavern-ously. "The greatest of all wizards and your eternal foe, Kull of Atlantis. You have won this tilt, but beware, there shall be others."

He burst the bonds on his arms with a single contemptuous gesture and stalked toward the door, the throng giving back before him.

"You are a fool of no discernment, Kull," said he. "Else you had never mistaken me for that other fool, Kuthulos, even with the veil and his garments."

Kull saw that it was so, for though the twain were alike in height and general shape, the flesh of the skull-faced wizard was like that of a man long dead.

The king stood, not fearful like the others, but so amazed at the turn of events that he was speechless. Then even as he sprang forward like a man waking from a dream, Brule charged with the silent ferocity of a tiger, his curved sword gleaming. And like a gleam of light it flashed into the ribs of Thulsa Doom, piercing him through and through, so that the point stood out between his shoulders.

Brule regained his blade with a quick wrench as he leaped back; then, crouching to strike again were it necessary, he halted. Not a drop of blood oozed from the wound which in a living man had been mortal. The skull-faced one laughed.

"Ages ago I died as men did!" he taunted. "Nay, I shall pass to some other sphere when my time comes, not before. I bleed not, for my veins are empty, and I feel only a slight coldness which shall pass when the wound closes, as it is even now closing. Stand back, fool, your master goes; but he shall come again to you, and you shall scream and shrivel and die in the coming! Kull, I salute you!"

And while Brule hesitated, unnerved, and Kull halted in undecided amazement, Thulsa Doom stepped through the door and vanished before their very eyes.

"At least, Kull," said Ka-nu later, "you have won your first tilt with the skull-faced one, as he admitted. Next time we must be more wary, for he is a fiend incarnate— an owner of magic black and unholy. He hates you, for he is a satellite of the great Serpent whose power you broke; he has the gift of illusion and of invisibility, which only he possesses. He is grim and terrible."

"I fear him not," said Kull. "The next time I will be prepared, and my answer shall be a sword thrust, even though he be unslayable, which thing I doubt. Brule did not find his vitals, which even a living dead man must have. That is all."

Then, turning to Tu: "Lord Tu, it would seem that the civilized races also have their tabus since the blue lake is forbidden to all save myself."

Tu answered testily, angry because Kull had given the happy Delcardes permission to marry whom she desired:

"My lord, that is no heathen tabu such as your tribe bows to; it is a matter of statecraft, to preserve peace between Valusia and the lake-beings, who are magicians."

"And we keep tabus so as not to offend unseen spirits of tigers and eagles," said Kull. "And therein I see no difference."

"At any rate," said Tu, "you must beware of Thulsa Doom, for he vanished into another dimension, and as long as he is there he is invisible and harmless to us; but he will come again."

"Ah, Kull," sighed the old rascal, Ka-nu, "mine is a hard life compared to yours; Brule and I were drunk in Zarfhaana, and I fell down a flight of stairs, most damnably bruising my shins. And all the while you lounged in sinful ease on the silk of the kingship, Kull."

Kull glared at him wordlessly and turned his back, giving his attention to the drowsing Saremes.

"She is not a wizard-beast, Kull," said the Spear-slayer. "She is wise, but she merely looks her wisdom and does not speak. Yet her eyes fascinate me with their antiquity. A mere cat, just the same."

"Still, Brule," said Kull, admiringly stroking her silky fur, "still, she is a very ancient cat. Very."

THE SKULL OF SILENCE

And a dozen death blots blotching him
On jowl and shank and huckle,
And he knocked on his skull with his knuckle,
And laughed—if you'd call it laughter—
At the billion facets of dying
In his outstart eyeballs shining.

Men still name it The Day of the King's Fear. For Kull, king of Valusia, was only a man after all. There was never a bolder man, but all things have their limits, even courage. Of course Kull had known apprehension and cold whispers of dread, sudden starts of horror, and even the shadow of unknown terror. But these had been but starts and leapings in the shadow of the mind, caused mainly by surprise or some loathsome mystery or unnatural thing—more repugnance than real fear. So real fear in him was so rare a thing that men mark the day.

Yet there was a time that Kull knew Fear, stark, terrible, and unreasoning, and his marrow weakened and his blood ran cold. So men speak of the time of Kull's Fear, and they do not speak in scorn, nor does Kull feel any shame. No, for as it came about, the thing rebounded to his undying glory.

Thus it came to be. Kull sat at ease on the Throne of

Society, listening idly to the conversation of Tu, chief councilor; Ka-nu, ambassador from Pictdom; Brule, Ka-nu's right-hand man; and Kuthulos the slave, who was yet the greatest scholar in the Seven Empires.

"All is illusion," Kuthulos was saying. "All outward manifestations of the underlying Reality, which is beyond human comprehension, since there are no relative things by which the finite mind may measure the infinite. The one may underlie all, or each natural illusion may possess a basic entity. All these things were known to Raama, the greatest mind of all the ages, who eons ago freed humanity from the grasp of unknown demons and raised the race to its heights."

"He was a mighty necromancer," said Ka-nu.

"He was no wizard," said Kuthulos. "No chanting, mumbling conjurer, divining from snake's livers. There was naught of mummery about Raama. He had grasped the First Principles; he knew the Elements and he understood that natural forces, acted upon by natural causes, produced natural results. He accomplished his apparent miracles by the exercise of his powers in natural ways, which were as simple in their manner to him as lighting a fire is to us, and as much beyond our ken as our fire would have been to our ape-ancestors."

"Then why did he not give all his secrets to the race?" asked Tu.

"He knew it is not good for man to know too much. Some villain would subjugate the whole race, nay, the whole universe, if he knew as much as Raama knew. Man must learn by himself and expand in soul as he learns."

"Yes, you say all is illusion," persisted Ka-nu, shrewd in statecraft, but ignorant in philosophy and science, and respecting Kuthulos or his knowledge. "How is that? Do we not hear and see and feel?"

"What is sight and sound?" countered the slave. "Is not sound the absence of silence, and silence absence of sound? The absence of a thing is not material substance. It is—nothing. And how can nothing exist?"

"Then why are things?" asked Ka-nu like a puzzled child.

"They are appearances of reality. Like silence; somewhere exists the essence of silence, the soul of silence. Nothing that is something; an absence so absolute that it takes material form. How many of you ever heard complete silence? None of us! Always there are some noises—the whisper of the wind, the flutter of an insect, even the growing of the grass, or on the desert, the murmur of the sands. But at the centre of silence, there is no sound."

"Raama," said Ka-nu, "long ago shut a spectre of silence into a great castle and sealed it there for all time."

"Aye," said Brule. "I have seen the castle: a great black thing on a lone hill, in a wild region of Valusia. Since time immemorial it has been known as the Skull of Silence."

"Ha!" Kull was interested now. "My friends, I would like to look upon this thing!"

"Lord king," said Kuthulos, "it is not good to tamper with what Raama made fast. For he was wiser than any man. I have heard the legend that by his arts he imprisoned a demon; not by his arts, say I, but by his knowledge of the natural forces, and not a demon but some element which threatened the existence of the race.

"The might of that element is evinced by the fact that not even Raama was able to destroy it; he only imprisoned it."

"Enough," Kull gestured impatiently. "Raama has been dead so many thousand years that it wearies me to think on it. I ride to find the Skull of Silence; who rides with me?"

All of those who listened to him, and a hundred of the Red Slayers, Valusia's mightiest war force, rode with Kull when he swept out of the royal city in the early dawn. They rode up among the mountains of Zalgara, and after many days' search they came upon a lone hill rising sombrely from the surrounding plateaus, and on its summit a great stark castle, black as doom.

"This is the place," said Brule. "No people live within a hundred miles of this castle, nor have they in the memory of man. It is shunned like a region accursed."

Kull reined his great stallion to a halt and gazed. No one spoke, and Kull was aware of the strange, almost intolerable stillness. When he spoke again, everyone started. To the king, it seemed that waves of deadening quiet emanated from that brooding castle on the hill. No birds sang in the surrounding land, and no wind moved the branches of the stunted trees. As Kull's horsemen rode up the slope, their footfalls on the rocks seemed to tinkle drearily and far away, dying without echo.

They halted before the castle that crouched there like a dark monster, and Kuthulos again essayed to argue with the king.

"Kull, consider! If you burst that seal, you may loose upon the world a monster whose might and frenzy no man can stay!"

Kull, impatient of restraint, waved him aside. He was in the grip of a wayward perverseness, a common fault of kings, and though usually reasonable, he had now made up his mind and was not to be swerved from his course.

"There are ancient writings on the seal, Kuthulos," he said. "Read them to me."

Kuthulos unwillingly dismounted, and the rest followed suit, all save the common soldiers who sat their horses like bronze images in the pale sunlight. The castle leered at them like a sightless skull, for there were no windows whatever and only one great door, that of iron and bolted and sealed. Apparently the building was all in one chamber.

Kull gave a few orders as to the disposition of the troops and was irritated when he found he was forced to raise his voice unseemingly in order for the commanders to understand him. Their answers came dimly and indistinctly.

He approached the door, followed by his four comrades. There on a frame beside the door hung a curious-appearing gong, apparently of jade, a sort of green in color. But Kull could not be sure of the color, for before his amazed stare it changed and shifted, and sometimes his gaze seemed to be drawn into depths and sometimes to glance at extreme shallowness. Beside the gong hung a mallet of the same strange material. He struck it lightly and then gasped, nearly stunned by the crash of sound which followed—it was like all earthly noise concentrated.

"Read the writings, Kuthulos," he commanded again, and the slave bent forward in considerable awe, for no doubt these words had been carved by the great Raama himself.

"That which was, may be again," he intoned. "Then beware, all sons of men!"

He straightened, a look of fright on his face.

"A warning! A warning straight from Raama! Mark ye, Kull, mark ye!"

Kull snorted, and drawing his sword, rent the seal from its hold and cut through the great metal bolt. He struck again and again, dimly aware of the comparative silence with which the blows fell. The bars fell, the door swung open.

Kuthulos screamed. Kull reeled, stared—the chamber was empty? *No!* He saw nothing, there was nothing to see, yet he felt the air throb about him as *something* came billowing from that foul chamber in great unseen waves. Kuthulos leaned to his shoulder and shrieked, and his words came faintly as from over cosmic distance.

"The Silence! This is the soul of all Silence!"

Sound ceased. Horses plunged and their riders fell face first into the dust and lay clutching at their heads with their hands, screaming without sound.

Kull alone stood erect, his futile sword thrust in front

of him. Silence! Utter and absolute! Throbbing, billowing waves of still horror. Men opened their mouths and shrieked, but there was no sound!

The Silence entered Kull's soul; it clawed at his heart; it sent tentacles of steel into his brain. He clutched at his forehead in torment; his skull was bursting, shattering. In the wave of horror which engulfed him, Kull saw red and colossal visions: the Silence spreading out over the Earth, over the Universe! Men died in gibbering stillness; the roar of rivers, the crash of seas, the noise of winds faltered and ceased to be. All Sound was drowned by the Silence. Silence, soul-destroying, brain-shattering; blotting out all life on Earth and reaching monstrously up into the skies, crushing the very singing of the stars!

And then Kull knew fear, horror, terror—overwhelming, grisly, soul-killing. Faced by the ghastliness of his vision, he swayed and staggered drunkenly, gone wild with fear. Oh gods, for a sound, the very slightest, faintest noise! Kull opened his mouth like the groveling maniacs behind him, and his heart nearly burst from his breast in his effort to shriek. The throbbing stillness mocked him. He smote against the metal sill with his sword. And still the billowing waves flowed from the chamber, clawing at him, tearing at him, taunting him like a being sensate with terrible Life.

Ka-nu and Kuthulos lay motionless. Tu writhed on his belly, his head in his hands, and squalled soundlessly like a dying jackal. Brule wallowed in the dust like a wounded wolf, clawing blindly at his scabbard.

Kull could almost see the form of the Silence now, the frightful Silence that was coming out of its Skull at last, to burst the skulls of men. It twisted, it writhed in the unholy wisps and shadows, it laughed at him! It lived! Kull staggered and toppled, and as he did, his outflung arm struck the gong. Kull heard no sound, but he felt a distinct throb and jerk of the waves about him, a slight withdrawal, involuntary, just as a man's hand jerks back from the flame.

Ah, old Raama left a safeguard for the race, even in death! Kull's dizzy brain suddenly read the riddle. The sea! The gong was like the sea, changing green shades, never still, now deep and now shallow, *never silent*.

The sea! Vibrating, pulsing, booming day and night; the greatest enemy of the Silence. Reeling, dizzy, nauseated, he caught up the jade mallet. His knees gave way, but he clung with one hand to the frame, clutching the mallet with the other in a desperate death grip. The Silence surged wrathfully about him.

Mortal, who are you to oppose me, who am older than the gods? Before Life was, I was, and shall be when Life dies. Before the invader Sound was born, the Universe was silent and shall be again. For I shall spread out through all the cosmos and kill Sound—kill Sound—kill Sound—kill Sound!

The roar of Silence reverberated through the caverns of Kull's crumbling brain in abysmal chanting monotones as he struck on the gong—again—and again—and again!

And at each blow the Silence gave back—inch by inch—inch by inch. Back, back, back. Kull renewed the force of his mallet blows. Now he could faintly hear the faraway tinkle of the gong, over unthinkable voids of stillness, as if someone on the other side of the Universe were striking a silver coin with a horseshoe nail. At each tiny vibration of noise, the wavering Silence started and shuddered. The tentacles shortened, and waves contracted. The Silence shrank.

Back and back and back—and back. Now the wisps hovered in the doorway, and behind Kull, men whimpered and wallowed to their knees, chins sagging and eyes vacant. Kull tore the gong from its frame and reeled toward the door. He was a finish fighter; no compromise for him. There would be no bolting the great door upon the horror again. The whole Universe should have halted to watch a man justifying the existence of mankind, scaling sublime heights of glory in his supreme atonement.

He stood in the doorway and leaned against the waves

that hung there, hammering ceaselessly. All Hell flowed out to meet him from the frightful thing whose very last stronghold he was invading. All of the Silence was now in the chamber again, forced back by the unconquerable crashings of Sound; Sound concentrated from all the sounds and noises of Earth and imprisoned by the master hand that long ago conquered both Sound and Silence.

And here Silence gathered all its forces for one last attack. Hells of soundless cold and noiseless flame whirled about Kull. Here was a thing, elemental and real. Silence was the absence of sound, Kuthulos had said: Kuthulos who now groveled and yammered empty nothingnesses.

Here was more than an absence, an absence whose utter absence became a presence, an abstract illusion that was a material reality. Kull reeled, blind, stunned, dumb, almost insensible from the onslaught of cosmic forces upon him; soul, body, and mind. Cloaked by the whirling tentacles, the noise of the gong died out again. But Kull never ceased. His tortured brain rocked, but he thrust his feet against the sill and shoved powerfully forward. He encountered material resistance, like a wave of solid fire, hotter than flame and colder than ice. Still he plunged forward and felt it give—give.

Step by step, foot by foot, he fought his way into the chamber of death, driving the Silence before him. Every step was screaming, demoniac torture; every foot was ravaging Hell. Shoulders hunched, head down, arms rising and falling in jerky rhythm, Kull forced his way, and great drops of blood gathered on his brow and dripped unceasingly.

Behind him, men were beginning to stagger up, weak and dizzy from the Silence that had invaded their brains. They gaped at the door, where the king fought his deathly battle for the Universe. Brule crawled blindly forward, trailing his sword, still dazed, and only following his stunned instinct which bade him follow the king, though the trail led to Hell.

Kull forced the Silence back, step by step, feeling it grow weaker and weaker, feeling it dwindle. Now the sound of the gong pealed out and grew and grew. It filled the room, the Earth, the sky. The Silence cringed before it, and as the Silence dwindled and was forced into itself, it took hideous form that Kull saw, yet did not see. His arms seemed dead, but with a mighty effort he increased his blows. Now the Silence writhed in a dark corner and shrank and shrank. Again, a last blow! All the sound in the Universe rushed together in one roaring, yelling, shattering, engulfing burst of sound! The gong flew into a million vibrating fragments. *And Silence screamed!*

BY THIS AXE I RULE!

1. "My Songs Are Nails for a King's Coffin!"

"At midnight the king must die!"

The speaker was tall, lean and dark; a crooked scar close to his mouth lent him an unusually sinister cast of countenance. His hearers nodded, their eyes glinting. There were four of these: a short fat man with a timid face, weak mouth, and eyes which bulged in an air of perpetual curiosity; a sombre giant, hairy and primitive; a tall, wiry man in the garb of a jester, whose flaming blue eyes flared with a light not wholly sane; and a stocky dwarf, abnormally broad of shoulders and long of arms.

The first speaker smiled in a wintry sort of manner. "Let us take the vow, the oath that may not be broken— the Oath of the Dagger and the Flame! I trust you; oh yes, of course. Still, it is better that there be assurance for all of us. I note tremors among some of you."

"That is all very well for you to say, Ardyon," broke in the short fat man. "You are an ostracized outlaw, anyway, with a price on your head; you have all to gain and nothing to lose, whereas we—"

"Have much to lose and more to gain," answered the outlaw imperturbably. "You called me down out of my mountain fastnesses to aid you in overthrowing a king. I have made the plans, set the snare, baited the trap, and stand ready to destroy the prey—but I must be sure of your support. Will you swear?"

"Enough of this foolishness!" cried the man with the blazing eyes. "Aye, we will swear this dawn, and tonight we will dance down a king! 'Oh, the chant of the chariots and the whir of the wings of the vultures.'"

"Save your songs for another time, Ridondo," laughed Ardyon. "This is a time for daggers, not rhymes."

"My songs are nails for a king's coffin!" cried the minstrel, whipping out a long, lean dagger. "Varlets, bring hither a candle! I shall be first to swear the oath!"

A silent and sombre slave brought a long taper, and Ridondo pricked his wrist, bringing blood. One by one, the other four followed his example, holding their wounded wrists carefully so that the blood should not drip yet. Then gripping hands in a circle, with the lighted candle in the centre, they turned their wrists so that the blood drops fell upon it. While it hissed and sizzled, they repeated:

"I, Ardyon, a landless man, swear the deep spoken and the silence covenanted, by the oath unbreakable."

"And I, Ridondo, first minstrel of Valusia's courts!" cried the minstrel.

"And I, Ducalon, count of Komahar," spoke the dwarf.

"And I, Enaros, commander of The Black Legion," rumbled the giant.

"And I, Kaanuub, baron of Blaal," quavered the short fat man in a rather tremulous falsetto.

The candle sputtered and went out, quenched by the ruby drops which fell upon it.

"So fades the life of our enemy," said Ardyon, releasing his comrades' hands. He looked on them with carefully veiled contempt. The outlaw knew that oaths may be broken, even "unbreakable" ones, but he knew also that Kaanuub, of whom he was most distrustful, was superstitious. There was no point in overlooking any safeguard, no matter how slight.

"Tomorrow," said Ardyon abruptly, "or rather, today,

for it is dawn now, Brule the Spear-slayer, the king's right hand man, departs for Grondar along with Ka-nu, the Pictish ambassador; the Pictish escort; and a goodly number of the Red Slayers, the king's bodyguard."

"Yes," said Ducalon with some satisfaction, "that was your plan, Ardyon, but I accomplished it. I have kin high in the council of Grondar and it was a simple matter to indirectly persuade the king of Grondar to request the presence of Ka-nu. And of course, as Kull honors Ka-nu above all others, he must have a sufficient escort."

The outlaw nodded.

"Good. I have at last managed, through Enaros, to corrupt an officer of the Red Guard. This man will march his men away from the royal bedroom tonight just before midnight, on a pretext of investigating some suspicious noise or the like. The various courtiers will have been disposed of. We will be waiting, we five, and sixteen desperate rogues of mine whom I have summoned from the hills, and who now hide in various parts of the city. Twenty-one against one—"

He laughed. Enaros nodded, Ducalon grinned, Kaanuub turned pale; Ridondo smote his hands together and cried out ringingly:

"By Valka, they will remember this night, who strike the golden strings! The fall of the tyrant, the death of the despot—what songs I shall make!"

His eyes burned with a wild fanatical light, and the others regarded him dubiously, all save Ardyon, who bent his head to hide a grin. Then the outlaw rose suddenly.

"Enough! Get back to your places and not by word, deed or look do you betray what is in your minds." He hesitated, eyeing Kaanuub. "Baron, your white face will betray you. If Kull comes to you and looks into your eyes with those icy gray eyes of his, you will collapse. Get you out to your country estate and wait until we send for you. Four are enough."

Kaanuub almost collapsed then, from a reaction of joy;

he left babbling incoherencies. The rest nodded to the outlaw and departed.

Ardyon stretched himself like a great cat and grinned. He called for a slave, and one came, a sombre-looking fellow whose shoulder bore the scars of the brand that marks thieves.

"Tomorrow," quoth Ardyon, taking the cup offered him, "I come into the open and let the people of Valusia feast their eyes upon me. For months now, ever since the Rebel Four summoned me from my mountains, I have been cooped in like a rat; living in the very heart of my enemies, hiding away from the light in the daytime, skulking, masked, through dark alleys and darker corridors at night. Yet I have accomplished what those rebellious lords could not. Working through them and through other agents, many of whom have never seen my face, I have honeycombed the empire with discontent and corruption. I have bribed and subverted officials, spread sedition among the people—in short, I, working in the shadows, have paved the downfall of the king who at the moment sits throned in the sun. Ah, my friend, I had almost forgotten that I was a statesman before I was an outlaw, until Kaanuub and Ducalon sent for me."

"You work with strange comrades," said the slave.

"Weak men, but strong in their ways," lazily answered the outlaw. "Ducalon—a shrewd man, bold, audacious, with kin in high places; but poverty-stricken, and his barren estates loaded with debts. Enaros—a ferocious beast, strong and brave as a lion, with considerable influence among the soldiers, but otherwise useless for he lacks the necessary brains. Kaanuub—cunning in his low way and full of petty intrigue, but otherwise a fool and a coward; avaricious but possessed of immense wealth which has been essential in my schemes. Ridondo—a mad poet, full of harebrained schemes, brave but flighty. A prime favorite with the people because of his songs which tear out their heartstrings. He is our best bid for popularity, once we have achieved our design."

"Who mounts the throne, then?"

"Kaanuub, of course—or so he thinks! He has a trace of royal blood in him, the blood of that king whom Kull killed with his bare hands. A bad mistake of the present king. He knows there are men who still boast descent from the old dynasty, but he lets them live. So Kaanuub plots for the throne. Ducalon wishes to be reinstated in favor as he was under the old regime, so that he may lift his estate and title to their former grandeur. Enaros hates Kelkor, commander of the Red Slayers, and thinks he should have that position. He wishes to be commander of all Valusia's armies. As for Ridondo—bah! I despise the man and admire him at the same time. He is your true idealist. He sees in Kull, an outlander and a barbarian, merely a rough-footed, red-handed savage who has come out of the sea to invade a peaceful and pleasant land. He already idolizes the king that Kull slew, forgetting the rogue's vile nature. He forgets the inhumanities under which the land groaned during his reign, and he is making the people forget. Already they sing "The Lament For the King" in which Ridondo lauds the saintly villain and vilifies Kull as "that black hearted savage." Kull laughs at these songs and indulges Ridondo, but at the same time wonders why the people are turning against him."

"But why does Ridondo hate Kull?"

"Because he is a poet, and poets always hate those in power and turn to dead ages for relief in dreams. Ridondo is a flaming torch of idealism, and he sees himself as a hero, a stainless knight rising to overthrow the tyrant."

"And you?"

Ardyon laughed and drained the goblet. "I have ideas of my own. Poets are dangerous things because they believe what they sing, at the time. Well, I believe what I think. And I think Kaanuub will not hold the throne overlong. A few months ago I had lost all ambitions save to waste the villages and the caravans as long as I lived. Now, well—now we shall see."

2. "Then I Was The Liberator—Now—"

A room strangely barren in contrast to the rich tapestries on the walls and the deep carpets on the floor. A small writing table, behind which sat a man. This man would have stood out in a crowd of a million. It was not so much because of his unusual size, his height and great shoulders, though these features lent to the general effect. But his face, dark and immobile, held the gaze, and his narrow gray eyes beat down the wills of the onlookers by their icy magnetism. Each movement he made, no matter how slight, betokened steel-spring muscles and brain knit to those muscles with perfect coordination. There was nothing deliberate or measured about his motions; either he was perfectly at rest—still as a bronze statue—or else he was in motion with that catlike quickness which blurred the sight that tried to follow his movements. Now this man rested his chin on his fists, his elbows on the writing table, and gloomily eyed the man who stood before him. This man was occupied in his own affairs at the moment, for he was tightening the laces of his breast-plate. Moreover he was abstractedly whistling, a strange and unconventional performance, considering that he was in the presence of a king.

"Brule," said the king, "this matter of statecraft wearies me as all the fighting I have done never did."

"A part of the game, Kull," answered Brule. "You are king; you must play the part."

"I wish that I might ride with you to Grondar," said Kull enviously. "It seems ages since I had a horse between my knees, but Tu says that affairs at home require my presence. Curse him!

"Months and months ago," he continued with increasing gloom, getting no answer, and speaking with freedom, "I overthrew the old dynasty and seized the throne of Valusia, of which I had dreamed ever since I was a boy in the land of my tribesmen. That was easy. Looking back now, over the long hard path I followed, all those days of toil, slaughter, and tribulation seem like so many dreams. From a wild tribesman in Atlantis, I rose, passing through the galleys of Lemuria—a slave for two years at the oars—then an outlaw in the hills of Valusia, then a captive in her dungeons, a gladiator in her arenas, a soldier in her armies, a commander, a king!

"The trouble with me, Brule, I did not dream far enough. I always visualized merely the seizing of the throne; I did not look beyond. When King Borna lay dead beneath my feet, and I tore the crown from his gory head, I had reached the ultimate border of my dreams. From there, it has been a maze of illusions and mistakes. I prepared myself to seize the throne, not to hold it.

"When I overthrew Borna, *then* people hailed me wildly; *then* I was The Liberator—*now* they mutter and stare blackly behind my back—they spit at my shadow when they think I am not looking. They have put a statue of Borna, that dead swine, in the Temple of the Serpent, and people go and wail before him, hailing him as a saintly monarch who was done to death by a red-handed barbarian. When I led her armies to victory as a soldier, Valusia overlooked the fact that I was a foreigner; now she cannot forgive me.

"And now, in the Temple of the Serpent, there come to burn incense to Borna's memory, men whom his executioners blinded and maimed, fathers whose sons died in his dungeons, husbands whose wives were dragged into his seraglio. Bah! Men are all fools."

"Ridondo is largely responsible," answered the Pict, drawing his sword-belt up another notch. "He sings songs that make men mad. Hang him in his jester's garb to the highest tower in the city. Let him make rhymes for the vultures."

Kull shook his leonine head. "No, Brule, he is beyond my reach. A great poet is greater than any king. He hates me; yet I would have his friendship. His songs are mightier than my sceptre, for time and again he has near torn the heart from my breast when he chose to sing for me. I will die and be forgotten; his songs will live forever."

The Pict shrugged his shoulders. "As you like; you are still king, and the people cannot dislodge you. The Red Slayers are yours to a man, and you have all Pictland behind you. We are barbarians together, even if we have spent most of our lives in this land. I go now. You have naught to fear save an attempt at assassination, which is no fear at all, considering the fact that you are guarded night and day by a squad of the Red Slayers."

Kull lifted his hand in a gesture of farewell, and the Pict clanked out of the room.

Now another man wished his attention, reminding Kull that a king's time was never his own.

This man was a young noble of the city, one Seno val Dor. This famous young swordsman and reprobate presented himself before the king with the plain evidence of much mental perturbation. His velvet cap was rumpled, and as he dropped it to the floor when he kneeled, the plume drooped miserably. His gaudy clothing showed stains as if in his mental agony he had neglected his personal appearance for some time.

"King, lord king," he said in tones of deep sincerity, "if the glorious record of my family means anything to your majesty, if my own fealty means anything, for Valka's sake, grant my request."

"Name it."

"Lord king, I love a maiden. Without her, I cannot live. Without me, she must die. I cannot eat, I cannot sleep for thinking of her. Her beauty haunts me day and night—the radiant vision of her divine loveliness—"

Kull moved restlessly. He had never been a lover.

"Then in Valka's name, marry her!"

"Ah," cried the youth, "there's the rub! She is a slave, Ala by name, belonging to one Ducalon, count of Komahar. It is on the black books of Valusian law that a noble cannot marry a slave. It has always been so. I have moved high heaven and get only the same reply. 'Noble and slave can never marry.' It is fearful. They tell me that never before in the history of the empire has a nobleman wanted to marry a slave. What is that to me? I appeal to you as a last resort."

"Will not this Ducalon sell her?"

"He would, but that would hardly alter the case. She would still be a slave, and a man cannot marry his own slave. Only as a wife do I want her. Any other way would be a hollow mockery. I want to show her to all the world rigged out in the ermine and jewels of val Dor's wife! But it cannot be, unless you can help me. She was born a slave, of a hundred generations of slaves, and slave she will be as long as she lives, and her children after her. And as such she cannot marry a freeman."

"Then go into slavery with her," suggested Kull, eyeing the youth narrowly.

"This I desired," answered Seno, so frankly that Kull instantly believed him. "I went to Ducalon and said, 'You have a slave whom I love; I wish to wed her. Take me, then, as your slave so that I may be ever near her.' He refused with horror; he would sell me the girl or give her to me, but he would not consent to enslave me. And my father has sworn on the unbreakable oath to kill me if I should so degrade the name of val Dor by going into slavery. No, lord king, only you can help me."

Kull summoned Tu and laid the case before him. Tu, chief councilor, shook his head. "It is written in the great iron-bound books, even as Seno has said. It has ever been the law, and it will always be the law. A noble may not mate with a slave."

"Why may I not change that law?" queried Kull.

Tu laid before him a tablet of stone whereon the law was engraved.

"For thousands of years this law has been. See, Kull, on the stone it was carved by the primal lawmakers, so many centuries ago a man might count all night and still not number them all. Not you, or any other king may alter it."

Kull felt suddenly the sickening, weakening feeling of utter helplessness which had begun to assail him of late. Kingship was another form of slavery, it seemed to him; he had always won his way by carving a path through his enemies with his great sword. How could he prevail against solicitous and respectful friends who bowed and flattered and were adamant against anything new; who barricaded themselves and their customs with tradition and antiquity and quietly defied him to change anything?

"Go," he said with a weary wave of his hand. "I am sorry, but I cannot help you."

Seno val Dor wandered out of the room, a broken man, if hanging head and bent shoulders, dull eyes and dragging steps mean anything.

3. "I Thought You a Human Tiger!"

A cool wind whispered through the green woodlands. A silver thread of a brook wound among great tree boles, whence hung large vines and gayly festooned creepers. A bird sang, and the soft late summer sunlight was sifted through the interlocking branches to fall in gold and black velvet patterns of shade and light on the grass-covered earth. In the midst of this pastoral quietude, a little slave girl lay with her face between her soft white arms, and wept as if her heart would break. The birds sang, but she was deaf; the brooks called her, but she was dumb; the sun shone, but she was blind—all the universe was a black void in which only pain and tears were real.

So she did not hear the light footfall nor see the tall, broad-shouldered man who came out of the bushes and stood above her. She was not aware of his presence until he knelt and lifted her, wiping her eyes with hands as gentle as a woman's.

The little slave girl looked into a dark immobile face, with cold, narrow gray eyes which just now were strangely soft. She knew this man was not a Valusian from his appearance, and in these troublous times it was not a good thing for little slave girls to be caught in the lonely woods by strangers, especially foreigners, but she was too miserable to be afraid, and, besides, the man looked kind.

"What's the matter, child?" he asked, and because a woman in extreme grief is likely to pour out her sorrows to anyone who shows interest and sympathy, she whimpered, "Oh, sir, I am a miserable girl. I love a young nobleman—"

"Seno val Dor?"

"Yes sir," she glanced at him in surprise. "How did you know? He wishes to marry me, and today, having striven in vain elsewhere for permission, he went to the king himself. But the king refused to aid him."

A shadow crossed the stranger's dark face. "Did Seno say the king refused?"

"No, the king summoned the chief councilor and argued with him awhile, but gave in. Oh," she sobbed, "I knew it would be useless! The laws of Valusia are unalterable, no matter how cruel or unjust. They are greater than the king."

The girl felt the muscles of the arms supporting her swell and harden into great iron cables. Across the stranger's face passed a bleak and hopeless expression.

"Aye," he muttered, half to himself, "the laws of Valusia are greater than the king."

Telling her troubles had helped her a little, and she

dried her eyes. Little slave girls are used to troubles and to suffering, though this one had been unusually kindly used all her life.

"Does Seno hate the king?" asked the stranger.

She shook her head. "He realizes the king is helpless."

"And you?"

"And I what?"

"Do you hate the king?"

Her eyes flared. "I! Oh, sir, who am I, to hate the king? Why, why, I never thought of such a thing."

"I am glad," said the man heavily. "After all, little one, the king is only a slave like yourself, locked with heavier chains."

"Poor man," she said, pityingly, though not exactly understanding; then she flamed into wrath. "But I do hate the cruel laws which the people follow! Why should laws not change? Time never stands still! Why should people today be shackled by laws which were made for our barbarian ancestors thousands of years ago—" She stopped suddenly and looked fearfully about.

"Don't tell," she whispered, laying her head in an appealing manner on her companion's shoulder. "It is not fit that a woman, and a slave girl at that, should so unashamedly express herself on such public matters. I will be spanked if my mistress or my master hears of it."

The big man smiled. "Be at ease, child. The king himself would not be offended by your sentiments; indeed, I believe that he agrees with you."

"Have you seen the king?" she asked, her childish curiosity overcoming her misery for the moment.

"Often."

"And is he eight feet tall," she asked eagerly, "and has he horns under his crown, as the common people say?"

"Scarcely," he laughed. "He lacks nearly two feet of answering your description as regards height; as for size, he might be my twin brother. There is not an inch difference in us."

"Is he as kind as you?"

"At times, when he is not goaded to frenzy by a state-craft which he cannot understand and by the vagaries of a people which can never understand him."

"Is he in truth a barbarian?"

"In very truth; he was born and spent his early boyhood among the heathen barbarians who inhabit the land of Atlantis. He dreamed a dream and fulfilled it. Because he was a great fighter and a savage swordsman, because he was crafty in actual battle, because the barbarian mercenaries in the Valusian army loved him, he became king. Because he is a warrior and not a politician, because his swordsmanship helps him now not at all, his throne is rocking beneath him."

"And he is very unhappy?"

"Not all the time," smiled the big man. "Sometimes when he slips away alone and takes a few hours holiday by himself among the woods, he is almost happy. Especially when he meets a pretty little girl like—"

The girl cried out in sudden terror, slipping to her knees before him. "Oh, sire, have mercy! I did not know; you are the king!"

"Don't be afraid." Kull knelt beside her again and put an arm about her, feeling her tremble from head to foot. "You said I was kind—"

"And so you are, sire," she whispered weakly. "I—I thought you were a human tiger, from what men said, but you are kind and tender—b-but—you are k-king, and I—"

Suddenly, in a very agony of confusion and embarrassment, she sprang up and fled, vanishing instantly. The realization that the king whom she had only dreamed of seeing at a distance some day, was actually the man to whom she had told her pitiful woes, overcame her with an abasement and embarrassment which was almost physical terror.

Kull sighed and rose. The affairs of the palace were calling him back, and he must return and wrestle with problems concerning the nature of which he had only

the vaguest idea, and concerning the solving of which he
had no idea at all.

4. "Who Dies First?"

Through the utter silence which shrouded the corridors and halls of the palace, twenty figures stole. Their
stealthy feet, cased in soft leather shoes, made no sound
either on thick carpet or bare marble tile. The torches
which stood in niches along the halls gleamed redly on
bared daggers, broadsword blade, and keen-edged axe.

"Easy, easy all!" hissed Ardyon, halting for a moment
to glance back at his followers. "Stop that cursed loud
breathing, whoever it is! The officer of the night guard
has removed all the guards from these halls, either by
direct order or by making them drunk, but we must be
careful. Lucky it is for us that those cursed Picts—the
lean wolves—are either reveling at the consulate or
riding to Grondar. Hist! back—here come the guard!"

They crowded back behind a huge pillar which might
have hidden a whole regiment of men, and waited.
Almost immediately, ten men swung by; tall brawny men
in red armor, who looked like iron statues. They were
heavily armed, and the faces of some showed a slight
uncertainty. The officer who led them was rather pale.
His face was set in hard lines, and he lifted a hand to
wipe sweat from his brow as the guard passed the pillar
where the assassins hid. He was young and this betraying
of a king came not easy to him.

They clanked by and passed on up the corridor.

"Good!" chuckled Ardyon. "He did as I bid; Kull
sleeps unguarded! Haste, we have work to do! If they
catch us killing him, we are undone, but a dead king is
easy to make a mere memory. Haste!"

"Aye, haste!" cried Ridondo.

They hurried down the corridor with reckless speed and stopped before a door.

"Here!" snapped Ardyon. "Enaros—break me open this door!"

The giant launched his mighty weight against the panel. Again—this time there was a rending of bolts, a crash of wood, and the door staggered and burst inward.

"In!" shouted Ardyon, on fire with the spirit of murder.

"In!" roared Ridondo. "Death to the tyrant—"

They halted short. Kull faced them—not a naked Kull, roused out of deep sleep, mazed and unarmed to be butchered like a sheep, but a Kull wakeful and ferocious, partly clad in the armor of a Red Slayer, with a long sword in his hand.

Kull had risen quietly a few minutes before, unable to sleep. He had intended to ask the officer of the guard into his room to converse with him awhile, but on looking through the spy-hole of the door, had seen him leading his men off. To the suspicious brain of the barbarian king had leaped the assumption that he was being betrayed. He never thought of calling the men back, because they were supposedly in the plot, too. There was no good reason for this desertion. So Kull had quietly and quickly donned the armor he kept at hand, nor had he completed this act when Enaros first hurtled against the door.

For a moment the tableau held—the four rebel noblemen at the door and the sixteen desperate outlaws crowding close behind them—held at bay by the terrible-eyed silent giant who stood in the middle of the royal bedroom, sword at the ready.

Then Ardyon shouted, "In and slay him! He is one to twenty, and he has no helmet!"

True, there had been lack of time to put on the helmet, nor was there now time to snatch the great shield from where it hung on the wall. Be that as it may, Kull was better protected than any of the assassins except

Enaros and Ducalon, who were in full armor with their vizors closed.

With a yell that rang to the roof, the killers flooded into the room. First of all was Enaros. He came in like a charging bull, head down, sword low for the disemboweling thrust. And Kull sprang to meet him like a tiger charging a bull, and all the king's weight and mighty strength went into the arm that swung the sword. In a whistling arc the great blade flashed through the air to crash down on the commander's helmet. Blade and helmet clashed and flew to pieces together, and Enaros rolled lifeless on the floor, while Kull bounded back, gripping the bladeless hilt.

"Enaros!" he snarled as the shattered helmet disclosed the shattered head; then the rest of the pack were upon him. He felt a dagger point rake along his ribs and flung the wielder aside with a swing of his left arm. He smashed his broken hilt square between another's eyes and dropped him senseless and bleeding to the floor.

"Watch the door, four of you!" screamed Ardyon, dancing about the edge of that whirlpool of singing steel, for he feared that Kull, with his great weight and speed, might crash through their midst and escape. Four rogues drew back and ranged themselves before the single door. And in that instant Kull leaped to the wall and tore therefrom an ancient battle-axe which had hung there for possibly a hundred years.

Back to the wall, he faced them for a moment; then leaped among them. No defensive fighter was Kull! He always carried the fight to the enemy. A sweep of the axe dropped an outlaw to the floor with a severed shoulder—the terrible backhand stroke crushed the skull of another. A sword shattered against his breastplate—else he had died. His concern was to protect his uncovered head and the spaces between breastplate and backplate, for Valusian armor was intricate, and he had not had time to fully arm himself. Already he was bleeding from wounds on the cheek and the arms and legs, but so swift and deadly was he, and so much the fighter, that even with the odds so greatly on their side, the assassins hesitated to leave an opening. Moreover, their own numbers hampered them.

For one moment they crowded him savagely, raining blows; then they gave back and ringed him, thrusting and parrying—a couple of corpses on the floor gave mute evidence of the folly of their first plan.

"Knaves!" screamed Ridondo in a rage, flinging off his slouch cap, his wild eyes glaring. "Do ye shrink from the combat? Shall the despot live? Out on it!"

He rushed in, thrusting viciously; but Kull, recognizing him, shattered his sword with a tremendous short chop and, with a push, sent him reeling back to sprawl on the floor. The king took in his left arm the sword of Ardyon, and the outlaw only saved his life by ducking Kull's axe and bounding backward. One of the bandits dived at Kull's legs, hoping to bring him down in that manner, but after wrestling for a brief instant at what seemed a solid iron tower, he glanced up just in time to see the axe falling, but not in time to avoid it. In the interim, one of his comrades had lifted a sword with both hands and hewed downward with such downright sincerity that he cut through Kull's shoulder plate on the left side, and wounded the shoulder beneath. In an instant the king's breastplate was full of blood.

Ducalon, flinging the attackers to right and left in his savage impatience, came plowing through and hacked savagely at Kull's unprotected head. Kull ducked and the sword whistled above, shaving off a lock of hair; ducking the blows of a dwarf like Ducalon is difficult for a man of Kull's height.

Kull pivoted on his heel and struck from the side, as a wolf might leap, in a wide level arc; Ducalon dropped with his entire left side caved in and the lungs gushing forth.

"Ducalon!" Kull spoke the word rather breathlessly. "I'd know that dwarf in Hell—"

He straightened to defend himself from the maddened rush of Ridondo, who charged in wide open, armed only with a dagger. Kull leaped back, axe high.

"Ridondo!" his voice rang sharply. "Back! I would not harm you—"

"Die, tyrant!" screamed the mad minstrel, hurling himself headlong on the king. Kull delayed the blow he was loath to deliver until it was too late. Only when he felt the bite of steel in his unprotected side did he strike, in a frenzy of blind desperation.

Ridondo dropped with a shattered skull, and Kull reeled back against the wall, blood spurting through the fingers which gripped his wounded side.

"In, now, and get him!" yelled Ardyon, preparing to lead the attack.

Kull placed his back to the wall and lifted his axe. He made a terrible and primordial picture. Legs braced far apart, head thrust forward, one red hand clutching at the wall for support, the other gripping the axe on high, while the ferocious features were frozen in a snarl of hate and the icy eyes blazed through the mist of blood which veiled them. The men hesitated; the tiger might be dying, but he was still capable of dealing death.

"Who dies first?" snarled Kull through smashed and bloody lips.

Ardyon leaped as a wolf leaps, halted almost in mid-air with the unbelievable speed which characterized him, and fell prostrate to avoid the death that was hissing toward him in the form of a red axe. He frantically whirled his feet out of the way and rolled clear just as Kull recovered from his missed blow and struck again; this time the axe sank four inches into the polished wood floor close to Ardyon's revolving legs.

Another desperado rushed at this instant, followed half-heartedly by his fellows. The first villain had figured on reaching Kull and killing him before he could get his axe out of the floor, but he miscalculated the king's speed, or else he started his rush a second too late. At any rate, the axe lurched up and crashed down, and the rush halted abruptly as a reddened caricature of a man was catapulted back against their legs.

At that moment a hurried clanking of feet sounded down the hall, and the rogues in the door raised a shout, "Soldiers coming!"

Ardyon cursed, and his men deserted him like rats leaving a sinking ship. They rushed out into the hall—or limped, splattering blood—and down the corridor a hue and cry was raised and pursuit started.

Save for the dead and dying men on the floor, Kull and Ardyon stood alone in the royal bedroom. Kull's knees were buckling, and he leaned heavily against the wall, watching the outlaw with the eyes of a dying wolf. In this extremity, Ardyon's cynical philosophy did not escape him.

"All seems to be lost, particularly honor," he murmured. "However, the king is dying on his feet, and—" Whatever other cogitation might have passed through his mind is not known, for at that moment he ran lightly at Kull just as the king was employing his axe arm to wipe the blood from his half-blind eyes. A man with a sword at the ready can thrust quicker than a wounded man, out of position, can strike with an axe that weights his weary arm like lead.

But even as Ardyon began his thrust, Seno val Dor appeared at the door and flung something through the air which glittered, sang, and ended its flight in Ardyon's throat. The outlaw staggered, dropped his sword, and sank to the floor at Kull's feet, flooding them with the flow of a severed jugular; mute witness that Seno's warskill included knife-throwing as well. Kull looked down bewilderedly at the dead outlaw, and Ardyon's dead eyes stared back in seeming mockery, as if the owner still maintained the futility of kings and outlaws, of plots and counterplots.

Then Seno was supporting the king, the room was flooded with men-at-arms in the uniform of the great val

Dor family, and Kull realized that a little slave girl was holding his other arm.

"Kull, Kull, are you dead?" val Dor's face was very white.

"Not yet," the king spoke huskily. "Staunch this wound in my left side; if I die 'twill be from it. It is deep— Ridondo wrote me a deathly song there!—but the rest are not mortal. Cram stuff into it for the present; I have work to do."

They obeyed wonderingly, and as the flow of blood ceased, Kull, though literally bled white already, felt some slight access of strength. The palace was fully aroused now. Court ladies, lords, men-at-arms, councilors, all swarmed about the place, babbling. The Red Slayers were gathering, wild with rage, ready for anything, jealous of the fact that others had aided their king. Of the young officer who had commanded the door guard, he had slipped away in the darkness, and neither then nor later was he in evidence, though earnestly sought after.

Kull, still keeping stubbornly to his feet, grasping his bloody axe with one hand and Seno's shoulder with another, singled out Tu, who stood wringing his hands, and ordered, "Bring me the tablet whereon is engraved the law concerning slaves."

"But lord king—"

"Do as I say!" yelled Kull, lifting the axe, and Tu scurried to obey.

As he waited, and the court women flocked about him, dressing his wounds and trying gently but vainly to pry his iron fingers from about the bloody axe handle, Kull heard Seno's breathless tale.

"—Ala heard Kaanuub and Ducalon plotting—she had stolen into a little nook to cry over her—our troubles, and Kaanuub came on his way to his country estate. He was shaking with terror for fear plans might go awry, and he made Ducalon go over the plot with him again before he left, so he might know there was no flaw in it.

"He did not leave until it was late in the evening, and only then did Ala find a chance to steal away and come to me. But it is a long way from Ducalon's city house to the house of val Dor, a long way for a little girl to walk, and though I gathered my men and came instantly, we almost arrived too late."

Kull gripped his shoulder.

"I will not forget."

Tu entered with the law tablet, laying it reverently on the table.

Kull shouldered aside all who stood near him and stood up alone.

"Hear, people of Valusia," he exclaimed, upheld by the wild beast vitality which was his. "I stand here—the king. I am wounded almost unto death, but I have survived mass wounds.

"Hear you! I am weary of this business. I am no king, but a slave! I am hemmed in by laws, laws, laws! I cannot punish malefactors nor reward my friends because of law—custom—tradition. By Valka, I will be king in fact as well as in name!

"Here stand the two who have saved my life. Henceforward they are free to marry, to do as they like."

Seno and Ala rushed into each other's arms with a glad cry.

"But the law!" screamed Tu.

"I am the law!" roared Kull, swinging up his axe; it flashed downward and the stone tablet flew into a hundred pieces. The people clenched their hands in horror, waiting dumbly for the sky to fall.

Kull reeled back, eyes blazing. The room whirled before his dizzy gaze.

"I am king, state, and law!" he roared, and seizing the wand-like sceptre which lay near, he broke it in two and flung it from him. "This shall be my sceptre!" The red axe was brandished aloft, splashing the pallid nobles with drops of blood. Kull gripped the slender crown with his left hand and placed his back against the wall; only that support kept him from falling, but in his arms was still the strength of lions.

"I am either king or corpse!" he roared, his corded muscles bulging, his terrible eyes blazing. "If you like not my kingship—come and take this crown!"

The corded left arm held out the crown, the right gripping the menacing axe above it.

"By this axe I rule! This is my sceptre! I have struggled and sweated to be the puppet king you wished me to be—to rule your way. Now I use mine own way. If you will not fight, you shall obey. Laws that are just shall stand, laws that have outlived their times I shall shatter as I shattered that one. *I am king!*"

Slowly the pale-faced noblemen and frightened women knelt, bowing in fear and reverence to the blood-stained giant who towered above them with his eyes ablaze.

"I am king!"

THE STRIKING OF THE GONG

Somewhere in the hot red darkness there began a throbbing. A pulsating cadence, soundless but vibrant with reality, sent out long rippling tendrils that flowed through the breathless air. The man stirred, groped about with blind hands, and sat up. At first it seemed to him that he was floating on the even and regular waves of a black ocean, rising and falling with monotonous regularity which hurt him physically somehow. He was aware of the pulsing and throbbing of the air and he reached out his hands as though to catch the elusive waves. But was the throbbing in the air about him, or in the brain inside his skull? He could not understand and a fantastic thought came to him—a feeling that he was locked inside his own skull.

The pulsing dwindled, centralized, and he held his aching head in his hands and tried to remember. Remember what?

"This is a strange thing," he murmured. "Who or what am I? What place is this? What has happened and why am I here? Have I always been here?"

He rose to his feet and sought to look about him. Utter darkness met his glance. He strained his eyes, but no single gleam of light met them. He began to walk forward, haltingly, hands out before him, seeking light as instinctively as a growing plant seeks it.

117

"This is surely not everything," he mused. "There must be something else—what is different from this? Light! I know—I remember Light, though I do not remember what Light is. Surely I have known a different world than this."

Far away a faint gray light began to glow. He hastened toward it. The gleam widened, until it was as if he were striding down a long and ever widening corridor. Then he came out suddenly into dim starlight and felt the wind cold in his face.

"This is light," he murmured, "but this is not all yet."

He felt and recognized a sensation of terrific height. High above him, even with his eyes, and below him, flashed and blazed great stars in a majestic glittering cosmic ocean. He frowned abstractedly as he gazed at these stars.

Then he was aware that he was not alone. A tall vague shape loomed before him in the starlight. His hand shot instinctively to his left hip, then fell away limply. He was naked and no weapon hung at his side.

The shape moved nearer and he saw that it was a man, apparently a very ancient man, though the features were indistinct and illusive in the faint light.

"You are new come here?" said this figure in a clear deep voice which was much like the chiming of a jade gong. At the sound a sudden trickle of memory began in the brain of the man who heard the voice.

He rubbed his chin in a bewildered manner.

"Now I remember," said he. "I am Kull, king of Valusia—but what am I doing here, without garments or weapons?"

"No man can bring anything through the Door with him," said the other cryptically. "Think, Kull of Valusia, know you not how you came?"

"I was standing in the doorway of the council chamber," said Kull dazedly, "and I remember that the watchman on the outer tower was striking the gong to denote the hour—then suddenly the crash of the gong merged into a wild and sudden flood of shattering sound. All went dark and red sparks flashed for an instant before my eyes. Then I awoke in a cavern or a corridor of some sort, remembering nothing."

"You passed through the Door; it always seems dark."

"Then I am dead? By Valka, some enemy must have been lurking among the columns of the palace and struck me down as I was speaking with Brule, the Pictish warrior."

"I have not said you were dead," answered the dim figure. "Mayhap the Door is not utterly closed. Such things have been."

"But what place is this? Is it Paradise or Hell? This is not the world I have known since birth. And those stars—I have never seen them before. Those constellations are mightier and more fiery than I ever knew in life."

"There are worlds beyond worlds, universes within and without universes," said the ancient. "You are upon a different planet than that upon which you were born; you are in a different universe, doubtless in a different dimension."

"Then I am certainly dead."

"What is death but a traversing of eternities and a crossing of cosmic oceans? But I have not said that you are dead."

"Then where in Valka's name am I?" roared Kull, his short stock of patience exhausted.

"Your barbarian brain clutches at material actualities," answered the other tranquilly. "What does it matter where you are, or whether you are dead, as you call it? You are part of that great ocean which is Life, which washes upon all shores, and you are as much a part of it in one place as in another, and as sure to eventually flow back to the Source of it, which gave birth to all Life. As for that, you are bound to Life for all Eternity as surely as a tree, a rock, a bird or a world is bound.

You call leaving your tiny planet, quitting your crude physical form—death!"

"But I still have my body."

"I have not said that you are dead, as you name it. As for that, you may be still upon your little planet, as far as you know. Worlds within worlds, universes within universes. Things exist too small and too large for human comprehension. Each pebble on the beaches of Valusia contains countless universes within itself, and itself as a whole is as much a part of the great plan of all universes, as is the sun you know. Your universe, Kull of Valusia, may be a pebble on the shore of a mighty kingdom.

"You have broken the bounds of material limitations. You may be in a universe which goes to make up a gem on the robe you wore on Valusia's throne or that universe you knew may be in the spiderweb which lies there on the grass near your feet. I tell you, size and space and time are relative and do not really exist."

"Surely you are a god?" said Kull curiously.

"The mere accumulation of knowledge and the acquiring of wisdom does not make a god," answered the other rather impatiently. "Look!" A shadowy hand pointed toward the great blazing gems which were the stars.

Kull looked and saw that they were changing swiftly. A constant weaving, an incessant changing of design and pattern was taking place.

"The 'everlasting' stars change in their own time, as swiftly as the races of men rise and fade. Even as we watch, upon those which are planets, beings are rising from the slime of the primeval, are climbing up the long slow roads to culture and wisdom, and are being destroyed with their dying worlds. All life and a part of life. To them it seems billions of years; to us, but a moment. All life."

Kull watched, fascinated, as huge stars and mighty constellations blazed and waned and faded, while others equally as radiant took their places, to be in turn supplanted.

Then suddenly the hot red darkness flowed over him again, blotting out all the stars. As through a thick fog, he heard a faint familiar clashing.

Then he was on his feet, reeling. Sunlight met his eyes, the tall marble pillars and walls of a palace, the wide curtained windows through which the sunlight flowed like molten gold. He ran a swift, dazed hand over his body, feeling his garments and the sword at his side. He was bloody; a red stream trickled down his temple from a shallow cut. But most of the blood on his limbs and clothing was not his. At his feet in a horrid crimson wallow lay what had been a man. The clashing he had heard ceased, re-echoing.

"Brule! What is this? What happened? Where have I been?"

"You had nearly been on a journey to old King Death's realms," answered the Pict with a mirthless grin as he cleansed his sword. "That spy was lying in wait behind a column and was on you like a leopard as you turned to speak to me in the doorway. Whoever plotted your death must have had great power to so send a man to his certain doom. Had not the sword turned in his hand and struck glancingly instead of straight, you had gone before him with a cleft skull, instead of standing here now mulling over a mere flesh wound."

"But surely," said Kull, "that was hours agone."

Brule laughed.

"You are still mazed, lord king. From the time he leaped and you fell, to the time I slashed the heart out of him, a man could not have counted the fingers of one hand. And during the time you were lying in his blood and yours on the floor, no more than twice that time elapsed. See, Tu has not yet arrived with bandages and he scurried for them the moment you went down."

"Aye, you are right," answered Kull. "I cannot understand—but just before I was struck down I heard the gong sounding the hour, and it was still sounding when I came to myself.

"Brule, there is no such thing as time nor space; for I have traveled the longest journey of my life, and have lived countless millions of years during the striking of the gong."

SWORDS OF THE PURPLE KINGDOM

1. "Valusia Plots Behind Closed Doors"

A sinister quiet lay like a shroud over the ancient city of Valusia. The heat waves danced from roof to shining roof and shimmered against the smooth marble walls. The purple towers and golden spires were softened in the faint haze. No ringing hoofs on the wide paved streets broke the drowsy silence, and the few pedestrians who appeared did what they had to do hastily and vanished indoors again. The city seemed like a realm of ghosts.

Kull, king of Valusia, drew aside the filmy curtains and gazed over the golden window sill, out over the court with sparkling fountains and trim hedges and pruned trees, over the high wall and at the blank windows of houses which met his glance.

"All Valusia plots behind closed doors, Brule," he grunted.

His companion, a dark-faced, powerful warrior of medium height, grinned hardly. "You are too suspicious, Kull. The heat drives most of them indoors."

"But they plot," reiterated Kull. He was a tall, broad-shouldered barbarian, with the true fighting build: wide shoulders, mighty chest, and lean flanks. Under heavy black brows his cold gray eyes brooded. His features

123

betrayed his birthplace, for Kull the usurper was an Atlantean.

"True, they plot. When did the people ever fail to plot, no matter who held the throne? And they might be excused now, Kull."

"Aye," the giant's brow clouded, "I am an alien. The first barbarian to press the Valusian throne since the beginning of time. When I was a commander of her forces they overlooked the accident of my birth. But now they hurl it into my teeth—by looks and thoughts, at least."

"What do you care? I am an alien also. Aliens rule Valusia now, since the people have grown too weak and degenerate to rule themselves. An Atlantean sits on her throne, backed by all the Picts, the empire's most ancient and powerful allies; her court is filled with foreigners; her armies with barbarian mercenaries; and the Red Slayers—well, they are at least Valusians, but they are men of the mountains who look upon themselves as a different race."

Kull shrugged his shoulders restlessly.

"I know what the people think, and with what aversion and anger the powerful old Valusian families must look on the state of affairs. But what would you have? The empire was worse under Borna, a native Valusian and a direct heir of the old dynasty, than it has been under me. This is the price a nation must pay for decaying: the strong young people come in and take possession, one way or another. I have at least rebuilt the armies, organized the mercenaries and restored Valusia to a measure of her former international greatness. Surely it is better to have one barbarian on the throne holding the crumbling bands together, than to have a hundred thousand riding red-handed through the city streets. Which is what would have happened by now, had it been left to King Borna. The kingdom was splitting under his feet, invasion threatened on all sides, the heathen Grondarians were ready to launch a raid of appalling magnitude—

"Well, I killed Borna with my bare hands that wild night when I rode at the head of the rebels. That bit of ruthlessness won me some enemies, but within six months I had put down anarchy and all counter-rebellions, had welded the nation back into one piece, had broken the back of the Triple Federation, and crushed the power of the Grondarians. Now Valusia dozes in peace and quiet, and between naps plots my overthrow. There has been no famine since my reign, the storehouses are bulging with grain, the trading ships ride heavy with cargo, the merchants' purses are full, the people are fat-bellied—but still they murmur and curse and spit on my shadow. What do they want?"

The Pict grinned savagely and with bitter mirth. "Another Borna! A red-handed tyrant! Forget their ingratitude. You did not seize the kingdom for their sakes, nor do you hold it for their benefit. Well, you have accomplished a lifelong ambition, and you are firmly seated on the throne. Let them murmur and plot. You are king."

Kull nodded grimly. "I am king of this purple kingdom! And until my breath stops and my ghost goes down the long shadow road, I will be king. What now?"

A slave bowed deeply. "Nalissa, daughter of the great house of bora Ballin, desires audience, most high majesty."

A shadow crossed the king's brow. "More supplication in regard to her damnable love affair," he sighed to Brule. "Mayhap you'd better go." To the slave, "Let her enter the presence."

Kull sat in a chair padded with velvet and gazed at Nalissa. She was only some nineteen years of age; and clad in the costly but scanty fashion of Valusian noble ladies, she presented a ravishing picture, the beauty of which even the barbarian king could appreciate. Her skin was a marvelous white, due partly to many baths in milk and wine, but mainly to a heritage of loveliness. Her cheeks were tinted naturally with a delicate pink, and her lips were full and red. Under delicate black brows brooded a pair of deep soft eyes, dark as mystery, and the whole picture was set off by a mass of curly black hair which was partly confined by a slim golden band.

Nalissa knelt at the feet of the king, and clasping his sword-hardened fingers in her soft slim hands, she looked up into his eyes; her own eyes luminous and pensive with appeal. Of all the people in the kingdom, Kull preferred not to look into the eyes of Nalissa. He saw there at times a depth of allure and mystery. She knew something of her powers, the spoiled and pampered child of aristocracy, but her full powers she little guessed because of her youth. But Kull, who was wise in the ways of men and women, realized with some uneasiness that with maturity Nalissa was bound to become a terrific power in the court and in the land, either for good or bad.

"But your majesty," she was wailing now, like a child begging for a toy, "please let me marry Dalgar of Farsun. He has become a Valusian citizen, he is high in favor at court, as you yourself say. Why—"

"I have told you," said the king with patience, "it is nothing to me whether you marry Dalgar, Brule, or the devil! But your father does not wish you to marry this Farsunian adventurer and—"

"But you can make him let me!" she cried.

"The house of bora Ballin I number among my staunchest supporters," answered the Atlantean. "And Murom bora Ballin, your father, among my closest friends. When I was a friendless gladiator, he befriended me. He lent me money when I was a common soldier, and he espoused my cause when I struck for the throne. Not to save this right hand of mine would I force him into an action to which he is so violently opposed, or interfere in his family affairs."

Nalissa had not yet learned that some men cannot be moved by feminine wiles. She pleaded, coaxed, and pouted. She kissed Kull's hands, wept on his breast, perched on his knee and argued, all much to his embarrassment, but to no avail. Kull was sincerely sympathetic, but adamant. To all her appeals and blandishments he had one answer: that it was none of his business, that her father knew better what she needed, and that he, Kull, was not going to interfere.

At last Nalissa gave up and left the presence with bowed head and dragging steps. As she emerged from the royal chamber, she met her father coming in. Murom bora Ballin, guessing his daughter's purpose in visiting the king, said nothing to her, but the look he gave her spoke eloquently of punishment to come. The girl climbed miserably into her sedan chair, feeling as if her sorrow was too heavy a load for any one girl to bear. Then her inner nature asserted itself. Her dark eyes smoldered with rebellion, and she spoke a few quick words to the slaves who carried her chair.

Count Murom stood before his king meanwhile, and his features were frozen into a mask of formal deference. Kull noted that expression, and it hurt him. Formality existed between himself and all his subjects and allies except the Pict, Brule; and the ambassador, Ka-nu; but this studied formality was a new thing in Count Murom, and Kull guessed at the reason.

"Your daughter was here, Count," he said abruptly.

"Yes, your majesty," the tone was impassive and respectful.

"You probably know why. She wants to marry Dalgar of Farsun."

The count made a stately inclination of his head. "If your majesty so wishes, he has but to say the word." His features froze into harder lines.

Kull, stung, rose and strode across the chamber to the window, where once again he gazed out at the drowsing city. Without turning, he said, "Not for half my kingdom would I interfere with your family affairs, nor force you into a course unpleasant to you."

The count was at his side in an instant, his formality vanished, his fine eyes eloquent. "Your majesty, I have wronged you in my thoughts—I should have known—" He made as if to kneel, but Kull restrained him.

The king grinned. "Be at ease, Count. Your private affairs are your own. I cannot help you, but you can help me. There is conspiracy in the air; I smell danger as in my early youth I sensed the nearness of a tiger in the jungle or a serpent in the high grass."

"My spies have been combing the city, your majesty," said the count, his eyes kindling at the prospect of action. "The people murmur as they will murmur under any ruler—but I have recently come from Ka-nu at the consulate, and he told me to warn you that outside influence and foreign money were at work. He said he knew nothing definite, but his Picts wormed some information from a drunken servant of the Verulian ambassador—vague hints at some coup that government is planning."

Kull grunted. "Verulian trickery is a byword. But Gen Dala, the Verulian ambassador, is the soul of honor."

"So much better a figurehead. If he knows nothing of what his nation plans, so much the better will he serve as a mask for their doings."

"But what would Verulia gain?" asked Kull.

"Gomlah, a distant cousin of King Gorna, took refuge there when you overthrew the old dynasty. With you slain, Valusia would fall to pieces. Her armies would become disorganized, all her allies except the Picts would desert her, the mercenaries whom only you can control would turn against her, and she would be an easy prey for the first powerful nation who might move against her. Then, with Gomlah as an excuse for invasion, as a puppet on Valusia's throne—"

"I see," grunted Kull. "I am better at battle than in council, but I see. So—the first step must be my removal, eh?"

"Yes, your majesty."

Kull smiled and flexed his mighty arms. "After all, this ruling grows dull at times." His fingers caressed the hilt of the great sword which he wore at all times.

"Tu, chief councilor to the king, and Dondal, his nephew," sang out a slave, and two men entered the presence.

Tu, chief councilor, was a portly man of medium height and late middle life, who looked more like a merchant than a councilor. His hair was thin, his face lined, and on his brow rested a look of perpetual suspicion. Tu's years and honors rested heavily on him. Originally of plebeian birth, he had won his way by sheer power of craft and intrigue. He had seen three kings come and go before Kull, and the strain told on him.

His nephew Dondal was a slim, foppish youth with keen dark eyes and a pleasant smile. His chief virtue lay in the fact that he kept a discreet tongue in his head and never repeated what he heard at court. For this reason he was admitted into places not even warranted by his close kinship to Tu.

"Just a small matter of state, your majesty," said Tu. "This permit for a new harbor on the western coast. Will your majesty sign?"

Kull signed his name; Tu drew from inside his bosom a signet ring attached to a small chain which he wore around his neck, and affixed the seal. This ring was the royal signature, in effect. No other ring in the world was exactly like it, and Tu wore it about his neck, waking or sleeping. Outside those in the royal chamber at the moment, not four men in the world knew where the ring was kept.

2. Mystery

The quiet of the day had merged almost imperceptibly into the quiet of night. The moon had not yet risen, and the small silver stars gave little light, as if their radiance was strangled by the heat which still rose from the earth.

Along a deserted street a single horse's hoofs clanged

hollowly. If eyes watched from the blank windows, they gave no sign that betrayed that anyone knew Dalgar of Farsun was riding through the night and the silence.

The young Farsunian was fully armed, his lithe athletic body was completely encased in light armor, and a morion was on his head. He looked capable of handling the long, slim jewel-hilted sword at his side, and the scarf which crossed his steel-clad breast, with its red rose, detracted nothing from the picture of manhood he presented.

Now as he rode he glanced at a crumpled note in his hand, which, half unfolded, disclosed the following message in the characters of Valusia: "At midnight, my beloved, in the Accursed Gardens beyond the walls. We will fly together."

A dramatic note; Dalgar's handsome lips curved slightly as he read. Well, a little melodrama was pardonable in a young girl, and the youth enjoyed a touch himself. A thrill of ecstasy shook him at the thought of that rendezvous. By dawn he would be far across the Verulian border with his bride-to-be; then let Count Murom bora Ballin rave; let the whole Valusian army follow their tracks. With that much start, he and Nalissa would be in safety. He felt high and romantic; his heart swelled with the foolish heroics of youth. It was hours until midnight, but—he nudged his horse with an armored heel and turned aside to take a shortcut through some dark narrow streets.

"Oh, silver moon and a silver breast—" he hummed under his breath the flaming love songs of the mad, dead poet Ridondo; then his horse snorted and shied. In the shadow of a squalid doorway, a dark bulk moved and groaned.

Drawing his sword, Dalgar slipped from the saddle and bent over him who groaned.

Bending very close, he made out the form of a man. He dragged the body into a comparatively lighter area, noting that he was still breathing. Something warm and sticky adhered to his hand.

The man was portly and apparently old, since his hair was sparse and his beard shot with white. He was clad in the rags of a beggar, but even in the darkness Dalgar could tell that his hands were soft and white under their grime. A nasty gash on the side of his head seeped blood, and his eyes were closed. He groaned from time to time.

Dalgar tore a piece from his sash to staunch the wound, and in so doing, a ring on his finger became entangled in the unkempt beard. He jerked impatiently—the beard came away entirely, disclosing the smooth-shaven, deeply lined face of a man in late middle life. Dalgar cried out and recoiled. He bounded to his feet, bewildered and shocked. A moment he stood, staring down at the groaning man; then the quick rattle of hoofs on a parallel street recalled him to life.

He ran down a side alley and accosted the rider. This man pulled up with a quick motion, reaching for his sword as he did so. The steel-shod hoofs of his steed struck fire from the flagstones as the horse set back on his haunches.

"What now? Oh, it's you, Dalgar."

"Brule!" cried the young Farsunian. "Quick! Tu, the chief councilor, lies in yonder side street, senseless—mayhap murdered!"

The Pict was off his horse in an instant, sword flashing into his hand. He flung the reins over his mount's head and left the steed standing there like a statue while he followed Dalgar on a run.

Together they bent over the stricken councilor while Brule ran an experienced hand over him.

"No fracture, apparently," grunted the Pict. "Can't tell for sure, of course. Was his beard off when you found him?"

"No, I pulled it off accidentally—"

"Then likely this is the work of some thug who knew him not. I'd rather think that. If the man who struck him down knew he was Tu, there's black treachery brewing in Valusia. I told him he'd come to grief prowling around the city disguised this way—but you cannot tell a councilor anything. He insisted that in this manner he learned all that was going on; kept his finger on the empire's pulse, as he said."

"But if it were a cutthroat," said Dalgar, "why did they not rob him? Here is his purse with a few copper coins in it—and who would seek to rob a beggar?"

The Spear-slayer swore. "Right. But who in Valka's name could know he was Tu? He never wore the same disguise twice, and only Dondal and a slave helped him with it. And what did they want, whoever struck him down? Oh well, Valka—he'll die while we stand here jabbering. Help me get him on my horse."

With the chief councilor lolling drunkenly in the saddle, upheld by Brule's steel-sinewed arms, they clattered through the streets to the palace. They were admitted by a wondering guard, and the senseless man was carried to an inner chamber and laid on a couch, where he was showing signs of recovering consciousness, under the ministrations of the slaves and court women.

At last he sat up and gripped his head, groaning. Ka-nu, Pictish ambassador and the craftiest man in the kingdom, bent over him.

"Tu! Who smote you?"

"I don't know." The councilor was still dazed. "I remember nothing."

"Had you any documents of importance about you?"

"No."

"Did they take anything from you?"

Tu began fumbling at his garments uncertainly; his clouded eyes began to clear, then flared in sudden apprehension. "The ring! The royal signet ring! It is gone!"

Ka-nu smote his fist into his palm and cursed soulfully.

"This comes of carrying the thing with you! I warned you! Quick, Brule, Kelkor—Dalgar; foul treason is afoot! Haste to the king's chamber."

In front of the royal bedchamber, ten of the Red Slayers, men of the king's favorite regiment, stood at guard. To Ka-nu's staccato questions, they answered that the king had retired an hour or so ago, that no one had sought entrance, and that they had heard no sound.

Ka-nu knocked on the door. There was no response. In a panic he pushed against the door. It was locked from within.

"Break that door down!" he screamed, his face white, his voice unnatural with unaccustomed strain.

Two of the Red Slayers, giants in size, hurled their full weight against the door, but it, being of heavy oak braced with bronze bands, held. Brule pushed them away and attacked the massive portal with his sword. Under the heavy blows of the keen edge, wood and metal gave way, and in a few moments Brule shouldered through the shreds and rushed into the room. He halted short with a stifled cry, and, glaring over his shoulder, Ka-nu clutched wildly at his beard. The royal bed was mussed as if it had been slept in, but of the king there was no sign. The room was empty, and only the open window gave hint of any clue.

"Sweep the streets!" roared Ka-nu. "Comb the city! Guard all the gates! Kelkor, rouse out the full force of the Red Slayers. Brule, gather your horsemen and ride them to death if necessary. Haste! Dalgar—"

But the Farsunian was gone. He had suddenly remembered that the hour of midnight approached, and of far more importance to him than the whereabouts of any king was the fact that Nalissa bora Ballin was awaiting him in the Accursed Gardens two miles beyond the city wall.

3. The Sign of the Seal

That night Kull had retired early. As was his custom, he halted outside the door of the royal bedchamber for a few minutes to chat with the guard, his old regimental mates, and exchange a reminiscence or so of the days when he had ridden in the ranks of the Red Slayers. Then, dismissing his attendants, he entered the chamber, flung back the covers of his bed, and prepared to retire. Strange proceedings for a king, no doubt, but Kull had been long used to the rough life of a soldier, and before that he had been a savage tribesman. He had never gotten used to having things done for him, and in the privacy of his bedchamber he would at least attend to himself.

But just as he turned to extinguish the candle which illumined his room, he heard a slight tapping at the window sill. Hand on sword, he crossed the room with the easy, silent tread of a great panther and looked out. The window opened on the inner grounds of the palace; the hedges and trees loomed vaguely in the semi-darkness of the starlight. Fountains glimmered vaguely, and he could not make out the forms of any of the sentries who paced those confines.

But here at his elbow was mystery. Clinging to the vines which covered the wall was a small wizened fellow who looked much like the professional beggars which swarmed the more sordid of the city's streets. He seemed harmless with his thin limbs and monkey face, but Kull regarded him with a scowl.

"I see I shall have to plant sentries at the very foot of my window, or tear these vines down," said the king. "How did you get through the guards?"

The wizened one put his skinny finger across puckered lips for silence; then with a simian-like dexterity, slid a hand through the bars. He silently handed Kull a piece of parchment. The king unrolled it and read: "King Kull: If you value your life, or the welfare of the kingdom, follow this guide to the place where he shall lead you. Tell no one. Let yourself be not seen by the guards. The regiments are honeycombed with treason, and if you are to live and hold the throne, you must do exactly as I say.

Trust the bearer of this note implicitly." It was signed "Tu, Chief Councilor of Valusia" and was sealed with the royal signet ring.

Kull knit his brows. The thing had an unsavory look— but this was Tu's handwriting—he noted the peculiar, almost imperceptible, quirk in the last letter of Tu's name, which was the councilor's trademark, so to speak. And then the sign of the seal, the seal which could not be duplicated. Kull sighed.

"Very well," he said. "Wait until I arm myself."

Dressed and clad in light chain-mail armor, Kull turned again to the window. He gripped the bars, one in each hand, and cautiously exerting his tremendous strength, felt them give until even his broad shoulders could slip between them. Clambering out, he caught the vines and swung down them with as much ease as was displayed by the small beggar who preceded him.

At the foot of the wall, Kull caught his companion's arm.

"How did you elude the guard?" he whispered.

"To such as accosted me, I showed the sign of the royal seal."

"That will scarcely suffice now," grunted the king. "Follow me; I know their routine."

Some twenty minutes followed of lying in wait behind a hedge or tree until a sentry passed, of dodging quickly into the shadows and making short, stealthy dashes. At last they came to the outer wall. Kull took his guide by the ankles and lifted him until his fingers clutched the top of the wall. Once astride it, the beggar reached down a hand to aid the king; but Kull, with a contemptuous gesture, backed off a few paces, took a short run, and bounding high in the air, caught the parapet with one upflung hand, swinging his great form up across the top of the wall with an almost incredible display of strength and agility.

The next instant the two strangely incongruous figures

had dropped down on the opposite side and faded into the gloom.

4. "Here I Stand at Bay!"

Nalissa, daughter of the house of bora Ballin, was nervous and frightened. Upheld by her high hopes and her sincere love, she did not regret her rash actions of the last few hours, but she earnestly wished for the coming of midnight and her lover.

Up to the present, her escapade had been easy. It was not easy for anyone to leave the city after nightfall, but she had ridden away from her father's house just before sundown, telling her mother that she was going to spend the night with a girl friend. It was well for her that women were allowed unusual freedom in the city of Valusia, and were not kept hemmed in seraglios and veritable prison houses as they were in the Eastern empires; a custom which survived the Flood.

Nalissa had ridden boldly through the eastern gate, and then made directly for the Accursed Gardens, two miles east of the city. These Gardens had once been the pleasure resort and country estate of a nobleman, but tales of grim debauches and ghastly rites of devil worship began to get abroad; and finally the people, maddened by the regular disappearance of their children, had descended on the Gardens in a frenzied mob and had hanged the prince to his own portals. Combing the Gardens, the people had found foul things, and in a flood of repulsion and horror had partially destroyed the mansion and the summer houses, the arbors, the grottoes, and the walls. But built of imperishable marble, many of the buildings had resisted both the sledges of the mob and the corrosion of time. Now, deserted for a hundred years, a miniature jungle had sprung up within the crumbling walls and rank vegetation overran the ruins.

Nalissa concealed her steed in a ruined summer house, and seated herself on the cracked marble floor, settling down to wait. At first it was not bad. The gentle summer sunset flooded the land, softening all scenes with its mellow gold. The green sea about her, shot with white gleams which were marble walls and crumbling roofs, intrigued her. But as night fell and the shadows merged, Nalissa grew nervous. The night wind whispered grisly things through the branches and the broad palm leaves and the tall grass, and the stars seemed cold and far away. Legends and tales came back to her, and she fancied that above the throb of her pounding heart she could hear the rustle of unseen black wings and the mutter of fiendish voices.

She prayed for midnight and Dalgar. Had Kull seen her then he would not have thought of her strange deep nature, nor the signs of her great future; he would have seen only a frightened little girl who passionately desired to be taken up and cuddled.

But the thought of leaving never entered her mind.

Time seemed as if it would never pass, but pass it did somehow. At last a faint glow betrayed the rising of the moon, and she knew the hour was closing to midnight.

Then suddenly there came a sound which brought her to her feet, her heart flying into her throat. Somewhere in the supposedly deserted Gardens there crashed into the silence a shout and a clang of steel. A short, hideous scream chilled the blood in her veins; then silence fell in a suffocating shroud.

Dalgar—Dalgar! The thought beat like a hammer in her dazed brain. Her lover had come and had fallen foul of someone—or something.

She stole from her hiding place, one hand over her heart which seemed about to burst through her ribs. She stole along a broken pave, and the whispering palm leaves brushed against her like ghostly fingers. About her lay a pulsating gulf of shadows, vibrant and alive with nameless evil. There was no sound.

Ahead of her loomed the ruined mansion; then without a sound, two men stepped into her path. She screamed once; then her tongue froze with terror. She tried to flee, but her legs would not work, and before she could move, one of the men had caught her up and tucked her under his arm as if she were a tiny child.

"A woman," he growled in a language which Nalissa barely understood, and which she recognized as Verulian. "Lend me your dagger and I'll—"

"We haven't time now," interposed the other, speaking in the Valusian tongue. "Toss her in there with him, and we'll finish them both together. We must get Phondar here before we kill him; he wants to question him a little."

"Small use," rumbled the Verulian giant, striding after his companion. "He won't talk—I can tell you that—he's opened his mouth only to curse us, since we captured him."

Nalissa, tucked ignominiously under her captor's arm, was frozen with fear, but her mind was working. Who was this "him" they were going to question and then kill? The thought that it must be Dalgar drove her own fear from her mind, and flooded her soul with a wild and desperate rage. She began to kick and struggle violently and was punished with a resounding smack that brought tears to her eyes and a cry of pain to her lips. She lapsed into a humiliated submission and was presently tossed unceremoniously through a shadowed doorway, to sprawl in a disheveled heap on the floor.

"Hadn't we better tie her?" queried the giant.

"What use? She can't escape. And she can't untie *him*. Hurry up; we've got work to do."

Nalissa sat up and looked timidly about. She was in a small chamber, the corners of which were screened with spider webs. Dust was deep on the floor, and fragments of marble from the crumbling walls littered it. Part of the roof was gone, and the slowly rising moon poured light through the aperture. By its light she saw a form on the floor, close to the wall. She shrank back, her teeth sinking into her lip with horrified anticipation; then she saw with a delirious sensation of relief that the man was too large to be Dalgar. She crawled over to him and looked into his face. He was bound hand and foot and gagged; above the gag, two cold gray eyes looked up into hers.

"King Kull!" Nalissa pressed both hands against her temples while the room reeled to her shocked and astounded gaze. The next instant her slim, strong fingers were at work on the gag. A few minutes of agonized effort, and it came free. Kull stretched his jaws and swore in his own language, considerate, even in that moment, of the girl's tender ears.

"Oh, my lord, how came you here?" The girl was wringing her hands.

"Either my most trusted councilor is a traitor or I am a madman!" growled the giant. "One came to me with a letter in Tu's handwriting, bearing even the royal seal. I followed him, as instructed, through the city and to a gate, the existence of which I had never known. This gate was unguarded and apparently unknown to any but they who plotted against me. Outside the gate, one awaited us with horses, and we came full speed to these damnable gardens. At the outer edge we left the horses, and I was led, like a blind, dumb fool for sacrifice, into this ruined mansion.

"As I came through the door, a great man-net fell on me, entangling my sword arm and binding my limbs, and a dozen rogues sprang on me. Well, mayhap my taking was not so easy as they had thought. Two of them were swinging on my already encumbered right arm so I could not use my sword, but I kicked one in the side and felt his ribs give way, and bursting some of the net's strands with my left hand, I gored another with my dagger. He had his death thereby and screamed like a lost soul as he gave up the ghost.

"But by Valka, there were too many of them. At last

they had me stripped of my armor,"—Nalissa saw the king wore only a sort of loincloth—"and bound as you see me. The devil himself could not break these strands; no, scant use to try to untie the knots. One of the men was a seaman, and I know of old the sort of knots they tie. I was a galley slave once, you know."

"But what can I do?" wailed the girl, wringing her hands.

"Take a heavy piece of marble and flake off a sharp sliver," said Kull swiftly. "You must cut these ropes—"

She did as he bid and was rewarded with a long thin piece of stone, the concave edge of which was as keen as a razor with a jagged edge.

"I fear I will cut your skin, sire," she apologized as she began work.

"Cut skin, flesh, and bone, but get me free!" snarled Kull, his eyes blazing. "Trapped like a blind fool! Oh, imbecile that I am! Valka, Honan, and Hotath! But let me get my hands on the rogues—how came you here?"

"Let us talk of that later," said Nalissa rather breathlessly. "Just now there is time for haste."

Silence fell as the girl sawed at the stubborn strands, giving no heed to her own tender hands, which were soon lacerated and bleeding. Slowly, strand by strand, the cords gave way; but there were still enough to hold the ordinary man helpless when a heavy step sounded outside the door.

Nalissa froze. A voice spoke, "He is within, Phondar, bound and gagged. With him is some Valusian wench that we caught wandering about the Gardens."

"Then be on watch for some gallant," spoke another voice, whose harsh, grating tones were those of a man accustomed to being obeyed. "Likely she was to meet some fop here. You—"

"No names, no names, good Phondar," broke in a silky Valusian voice. "Remember our agreement; until Gomlah mounts the throne, I am simply—the Masked One."

"Very good," grunted the Verulian. "You have done a

good night's work, Masked One. None but you could have done it, for only you knew how to obtain the royal signet. Only you could so closely counterfeit Tu's writing—by the way, did you kill the old fellow?"

"What matter? Tonight, or the day Gomlah mounts the throne, he dies. The matter of most importance is that the king lies helpless in our power."

Kull was racking his brain trying to place the hauntingly familiar voice of the traitor. And Phondar—his face grew grim. A deep conspiracy indeed, if Verulia must send the commander of her royal armies to do her foul work. The king knew Phondar well, and had aforetime entertained him in the palace.

"Go in and bring him out," said Phondar. "We will take him to the old torture chamber. I have questions to ask of him."

The door opened, admitting one man: the giant who had captured Nalissa. The door closed behind him and he crossed the room, giving scarcely a glance to the girl who cowered in a corner. He bent over the bound king, took him by leg and shoulder to lift him bodily; there came a sudden loud snap as Kull, throwing all his iron strength into one convulsive wrench, broke the remaining strands which bound him.

He had not been tied long enough for all circulation to be cut off and his strength affected thereby. As a python strikes, his hands shot to the giant's throat; shot, and gripped like a steel vise.

The giant went to his knees. One hand flew to the fingers at his throat, the other to his dagger. His fingers sank like steel into Kull's wrist, the dagger flashed from its sheath; then his eyes bulged, his tongue sagged out. The fingers fell away from the king's wrist, and the dagger slipped from a nerveless grip. The Verulian went limp, his throat literally crushed in that terrible grip. Kull, with one terrific wrench, broke his neck and, releasing him, tore the sword from its sheath. Nalissa had picked up the dagger.

The combat had taken only a few flashing seconds and had caused no more noise than might have resulted from a man lifting and shouldering a great weight.

"Hasten!" called Phondar's voice impatiently from beyond the door, and Kull, crouching tigerlike just inside, thought quickly. He knew that there were at least a score of conspirators in the Gardens. He knew also, from the sound of voices, that there were only two or three outside the door at the moment. This room was not a good place to defend. In a moment they would be coming in to see what occasioned the delay. He reached a decision and acted promptly.

He beckoned the girl. "As soon as I have gone through the door, run out likewise and go up the stairs which lead away to the left." She nodded, trembling, and he patted her slim shoulder reassuringly. Then he whirled and flung open the door.

To the men outside, expecting the Verulian giant with the helpless king on his shoulders, appeared an apparition which was dumbfounding in its unexpectedness. Kull stood in the door; Kull, half-naked, crouching like a great human tiger, his teeth bared in a snarl of battle fury, his eyes blazing. His sword blade whirled like a wheel of silver in the moonlight.

Kull saw Phondar, two Verulian soldiers, a slim figure in a black mask—a flashing instant, and then he was among them and the dance of death was on. The Verulian commander went down in the king's first lunge, his head cleft to the teeth in spite of his helmet. The Masked One drew and thrust, his point raking Kull's cheek; one of the soldiers drove at the king with a spear, was parried, and the next instant lay dead across his master. The remaining soldier broke and ran, yelling lustily for his comrades. The Masked One retreated swiftly before the headlong attack of the king, parrying and guarding with an almost uncanny skill. He had no time to launch an attack of his own; before the whirlwind ferocity of Kull's charge he had only time for defense. Kull beat against his blade like a blacksmith on an anvil, and again and again it seemed as though the long Verulian steel must inevitably cleave that masked and hooded head, but always the long slim Valusian sword was in the way, turning the blow by an inch or stopping it within a hair's-breadth of the skin, but always just enough.

Then Kull saw the Verulian soldiers running through the foliage and heard the clang of their weapons and their fierce shouts. Caught here in the open, they would get behind him and slit him like a rat. He slashed once more, viciously, at the retreating Valusian, and then, backing away, turned and ran fleetly up the stairs, at the top of which Nalissa already stood.

There he turned at bay. He and the girl stood on a sort of artificial promontory. A stair led up, and a stair had once led down the other way, but now the back stair had long since crumbled away. Kull saw that they were in a cul-de-sac. The walls were cut deep with ornate carvings but— *Well*, thought Kull, *here we die. But here many others die, too*.

The Verulians were gathering at the foot of the stair, under the leadership of the mysterious masked Valusian. Kull took a fresh grip on his sword hilt and flung back his head, an unconscious reversion to days when he had worn a lion-like mane of hair.

Kull had never feared death; he did not fear it now, and, except for one consideration, he would have welcomed the clamor and madness of battle as an old friend, without regrets. This consideration was the girl who stood beside him. As he looked at her trembling form and white face, he reached a sudden decision.

He raised his hand and shouted, "Ho, men of Verulia! Here I stand at bay. Many shall fall before I die. But promise me to release the girl, unharmed, and I will not lift a hand. You may then kill me like a sheep."

Nalissa cried in protest, and the Masked One laughed. "We make no bargains with one already doomed. The girl also must die, and I make no promises to be broken. Up, warriors, and take him!"

They flooded the stair like a black wave of death, swords sparkling like frosty silver in the moonlight. One was far in advance of his fellows, a huge warrior who bore on high a great battle-axe. Moving quicker than Kull had anticipated, this man was on the landing in an instant. Kull rushed in, and the axe descended. He caught the heavy shaft with his left hand and checked the downward rush of the weapon in mid-air—a feat few men could have done—and at the same time struck in from the side with his right, a sweeping hammerlike blow which sent the long sword crunching through armor, muscle, and bone, and left the broken blade wedged in the spinal column.

At the same instant, he released the useless hilt and tore the axe from the nerveless grasp of the dying warrior, who pitched back down the stairs. And Kull laughed shortly and grimly.

The Verulians hesitated on the stair, and, below, the Masked One savagely urged them on. They were inclined to be rebellious.

"Phondar is dead," shouted one. "Shall we take orders from this Valusian? This is a devil and not a man who faces us! Let us save ourselves!"

"Fools!" the Masked One's voice rose in a ferine shriek. "Don't you see that your own safety lies in slaying the king? If you fail tonight, your own government will repudiate you and will aid the Valusians in hunting you down! Up, fools! You will die, some of you, but better for a few to die under the king's axe than for all to die on the gibbet! Let one man retreat down these stairs— that man will I kill!" And the long, slender sword menaced them.

Desperate, afraid of their leader, and recognizing the truth of his words, the score or more of warriors turned their breasts to Kull's steel. As they massed for what must necessarily be the last charge, Nalissa's attention was attracted by a movement at the base of the wall. A shadow detached itself from the rest of the shadows and moved up the sheer face of the wall, climbing like an ape and using the deep carvings for foot and hand holds. This side of the wall was in shadow, and she could not make out the features of the man; moreover, he wore a heavy morion which shaded his face.

Saying nothing to Kull, who stood at the landing, his axe poised, she stole over to the edge of the wall, half concealing herself behind a ruin of what had once been a parapet. Now she could see that the man was in full armor, but still she could not make out his features. Her breath came fast, and she raised the dagger, fighting fiercely to overcome a tendency of nausea.

Now a steel-clad arm hooked up over the edge—she sprang as quickly and silently as a tigress and struck full at the unprotected face suddenly upturned in the moonlight. And even as the dagger fell, and she was unable to check the blow, she screamed, wildly and agonizedly. For in that fleeting second, she recognized the face of her lover, Dalgar of Farsun.

5. The Battle of the Stair

Dalgar, after unceremoniously leaving the distracted presence of Ka-nu, ran to his horse and rode hard for the eastern gate. He had heard Ka-nu give orders to close the gates and let no one out, and he rode like a madman to beat that order. It was a hard matter to get out at night anyway, and Dalgar, having learned that the gates were not guarded tonight by the incorruptible Red Slayers, had planned to bribe his way out. Now he depended upon the audacity of his scheme.

All in a lather of sweat, he halted at the eastern gate and shouted, "Unbolt the gate! I must ride to the Verulian border tonight! Quickly! The king has vanished! Let me through and then guard the gate! In the name of the king!"

Then, as the soldier hesitated, "Haste, fools! The king may be in mortal danger! Hark!"

Far out across the city, chilling hearts with sudden nameless dread, sounded the deep tones of the great bronze Bell of the King, which booms only when the king is in peril. The guards were electrified. They knew Dalgar was high in favor as a visiting noble. They believed what he said, so, under the impetuous blast of his will, they swung the great iron gates wide, and he shot through like a thunderbolt to vanish instantly in the outer darkness.

As Dalgar rode, he hoped no great harm had come to Kull, for he liked the bluff barbarian far more than he had ever liked any of the sophisticated and bloodless kings of the Seven Empires. Had it been possible, he would have aided in the search. But Nalissa was waiting for him, and already he was late.

As the young nobleman entered the Gardens, he had a peculiar feeling that here in the heart of desolation and loneliness there were many men. An instant later he heard a clash of steel, the sound of many running footsteps, and a fierce shouting in a foreign tongue. Slipping off his horse and drawing his sword, he crept through the underbrush until he came in sight of the ruined mansion. There a strange sight burst upon his vision. At the top of the crumbling staircase stood a half-naked, blood-stained giant whom he recognized as the king of Valusia. By his side stood a girl—a half-stifled cry burst from Dalgar's lips. Nalissa! His nails bit into the palms of his clenched hand. Who were those men in dark clothing who swarmed up the stairs? No matter. They meant death to the girl and to Kull. He heard the king challenge them and offer his life for Nalissa's, and a flood of gratitude engulfed him. Then he noted the deep carvings on the wall nearest him. The next instant he was climbing, to die by the side of the king, protecting the girl he loved.

He had lost sight of Nalissa, and now as he climbed he dared not take the time to look up for her. This was a slippery and treacherous task. He did not see her until he caught hold of the edge to pull himself up; then he heard her scream and saw her hand falling toward his face, gripping a gleam of silver. He ducked and took the blow on his morion; the dagger snapped at the hilt, and Nalissa collapsed in his arms the next moment.

Kull had whirled, axe high, at her scream; now he paused. He recognized the Farsunian, and even in that instant he read between the lines. He knew why the couple were here and grinned with real enjoyment.

A second charge had halted, as the Verulians had noted the second man on the landing; now they came on again, bounding up the steps in the moonlight, blades gleaming, eyes wild with desperation. Kull met the first with an overhand smash that crushed helmet and skull; then Dalgar was at his side, and his blade licked out and into a Verulian throat. Then began the battle of the stair, since immortalized by singers and poets.

Kull was there to die and slay before he died. He gave scant thought to defense. His axe played a wheel of death about him, and with each blow there came a crunch of steel and bone, a spurt of blood, a gurgling cry of agony. Bodies choked the wide stair, but still the survivors came, clambering over the gory forms of their comrades.

Dalgar had little opportunity to thrust or cut. He had seen in an instant that his best task lay in protecting Kull, who was a born killer, but who, in his armorless condition, was likely to fall at any instant.

So Dalgar wove a web of steel about the king, bringing into play all the sword skill that was his. Again and again his flashing blade turned a point from Kull's heart; again and again his mail-clad forearm intercepted a blow that else had killed. Twice he took on his own helmet slashes meant for the king's bare head.

It is not easy to guard another man and yourself at the same time. Kull was bleeding from cuts on the face and breast, from a gash above the temple, a stab in the thigh, and a deep wound in the left shoulder; a thrusting pike had rent Dalgar's cuirass and wounded him in the side, and he felt his strength ebbing. A last mad effort of their foes and the Farsunian was overthrown. He fell at Kull's feet, and a dozen points prodded for his life. With a lion-like roar, Kull cleared a space with one mighty sweep of his red axe and stood astride the fallen youth. They closed in—

There burst on Kull's ears a crash of horses' hoofs and the Accursed Gardens were flooded with wild riders, yelling like wolves in the moonlight. A storm of arrows swept the stairs, and men howled, pitching headlong to lie still, or to tear at the cruel, deeply embedded shafts. The few whom Kull's axe and the arrows had left fled down the stairs to be met at the bottom by the whistling curved swords of Brule's Picts. And there they died, fighting to the last, those bold Verulian warriors—cat's-paws for their false king, sent out on a dangerous and foul mission, disowned by the men who sent them out, and branded forever with infamy. But they died like men.

But one did not die there at the foot of the stairs. The Masked One had fled at the first sound of hoofs, and now he shot across the Gardens riding a superb horse. He had almost reached the outer wall when Brule, the Spear-slayer, dashed across his path. There on the promontory, leaning on his bloody axe, Kull saw them fight beneath the moon.

The Masked One had abandoned his defensive tactics. He charged the Pict with reckless courage, and the Spear-slayer met him, horse to horse, man to man, blade to blade. Both were magnificent horsemen. Their steeds, obeying the touch of the bridle, the nudge of the knee, whirled, reared, and spun. But through all their motions, the whistling blades never lost touch of each other. Brule, unlike his tribesmen, used the slim straight sword of Valusia. In reach and speed there was little difference between them, and Kull, watching, again and again caught his breath and bit his lip as it seemed Brule would fall before an unusually vicious thrust.

No crude hacking and slashing for these seasoned warriors. They thrust and countered, parried and thrust again. Then suddenly Brule seemed to lose touch with his opponent's blade—he parried wildly, leaving himself wide open—the Masked One struck heels into his horse's side as he lunged, so that the sword and horse shot forward as one. Brule leaned aside, let the blade glance from the side of his cuirass; his own blade shot straight out, elbow, wrist, hilt, and point making a straight line from his shoulder. The horses crashed together and together they rolled headlong on the sward. But from that tangle of lashing hoofs Brule rose unharmed, while there in the grass lay the Masked One, Brule's sword still transfixing him.

Kull awoke as from a trance; the Picts were howling about like wolves, but he raised his hand for silence. "Enough! You are all heroes! But attend to Dalgar; he is sorely wounded. And when you have finished, you might see to my own wounds. Brule, how came you to find me?"

Brule beckoned Kull to where he stood above the dead Masked One.

"A beggar crone saw you climb the palace wall, and out of curiosity watched where you went. She followed and saw you go through the forgotten gate. I was riding the plain between the wall and these Gardens when I heard the clash of steel. But who can this be?"

"Raise the mask," said Kull. "Whoever it is, it is he who copied Tu's handwriting, who took the signet ring from Tu, and—"

Brule tore the mask away.

"Dondal!" Kull ejaculated. "Tu's nephew! Brule, Tu must never know this. Let him think that Dondal rode with you and died fighting for his king."

Brule seemed stunned. "Dondal! A traitor! Why, many

a time I've drunk wine with him and slept it off in one of his beds."

Kull nodded. "I liked Dondal."

Brule cleansed his blade and drove it home in the scabbard with a vicious clank. "Want will make a rogue of any man," he said moodily. "He was deep in debt— Tu was penurious with him. Always maintained that giving young men money was bad for them. Dondal was forced to keep up appearances for his pride's sake, and so fell into the hands of the usurers. Thus Tu is the greater traitor, for he drove the boy into treachery by his parsimony—and I could wish Tu's heart had stopped my point instead of his."

So saying, the Pict turned on his heel and strode sombrely away.

Kull turned back to Dalgar, who lay half-senseless while the Pictish warriors dressed his wounds with experienced fingers. Others attended to the king, and while they staunched, cleansed, and bandaged, Nalissa came up to Kull.

"Sire," she held out her small hands, now scratched and stained with dried blood, "will you now have mercy on us—grant my plea if—" her voice caught on a sob— "if Dalgar lives?"

Kull caught her slim shoulders and shook her in his anguish.

"Girl, girl, girl! Ask me anything except something I cannot grant. Ask half my kingdom or my right hand, and it is yours. I will ask Murom to let you marry Dalgar—I will beg him—but I cannot force him."

Tall horsemen were gathering through the Gardens, whose resplendent armor shone among the half-naked, wolfish Picts. A tall man hurried up, throwing back the vizor of his helmet.

"Father!"

Murom bora Ballin crushed his daughter to his breast with a sob of thanksgiving, and then turned to *his* king.

"Sire, you are sorely wounded!"

Kull shook his head. "Not sorely; at least, not for me, though other men might feel stiff and sore. But yonder lies he who took the death thrusts meant for me; who was my shield and my helmet, and but for whom Valusia had howled for a new king."

Murom whirled toward the prostrate youth.

"Dalgar! Is he dead?"

"Nigh unto it," growled a wiry Pict who was still working above him. "But he is steel and whalebone; with any care he should live."

"He came here to meet your daughter and elope with her," said Kull, while Nalissa hung her head. "He crept through the brush and saw me fighting for my life and hers, atop yonder stair. He might have escaped. Nothing barred him. But he climbed the sheer wall to certain death, as it seemed then, and fought by my side as gayly as he ever rode to a feast—and he not even a subject of mine by birth."

Murom's hands clenched and unclenched. His eyes kindled and softened as they bent on his daughter.

"Nalissa," he said softly, drawing the girl into the shelter of his steel-clad arm, "do you still wish to marry this reckless youth?"

Her eyes spoke eloquently enough.

Kull was speaking, "Take him up carefully and bear him to the palace; he shall have the best—"

Murom interposed, "Sire, if I may ask; let him be taken to my castle. There the finest physicians shall attend him and on his recovery—well, if it be your royal pleasure, might we not celebrate the event with a wedding?"

Nalissa screamed with joy, clapped her hands, kissed her father and Kull, and was off to Dalgar's side like a whirlwind.

Murom smiled softly, his aristocratic face alight.

"Out of a night of blood and terror, joy and happiness are born."

The barbarian king grinned and shouldered his stained and notched axe.

"Life is that way, Count; one man's bane is another's bliss."

THE MIRRORS OF TUZUN THUNE

"A wild, weird clime that lieth sublime
Out of Space, out of Time."

—POE

There comes, even to kings, the time of great weariness. Then the gold of the throne is brass, the silk of the palace becomes drab. The gems in the diadem sparkle drearily like the ice of the white seas; the speech of men is as the empty rattle of a jester's bell and the feel comes of things unreal; even the sun is copper in the sky, and the breath of the green ocean is no longer fresh.

Kull sat upon the throne of Valusia and the hour of weariness was upon him. They moved before him in an endless, meaningless panorama: men, women, priests, events and shadows of events; things seen and things to be attained. But like shadows they came and went, leaving no trace upon his consciousness, save that of a great mental fatigue. Yet Kull was not tired. There was a longing in him for things beyond himself and beyond the Valusian court. An unrest stirred in him, and strange, luminous dreams roamed his soul. At his bidding there came to him Brule the Spear-slayer, warrior of Pictland, from the islands beyond the West.

"Lord king, you are tired of the life of the court. Come

with me upon my galley and let us roam the tides for a space."

"Nay." Kull rested his chin moodily upon his mighty hand. "I am weary beyond all these things. The cities hold no lure for me—and the borders are quiet. I hear no more the sea-songs I heard when I lay as a boy on the booming crags' of Atlantis, and the night was alive with blazing stars. No more do the green woodlands beckon me as of old. There is a strangeness upon me and a longing beyond life's longings. Go!"

Brule went forth in a doubtful mood, leaving the king brooding upon his throne. Then to Kull stole a girl of the court and whispered:

"Great king, seek Tuzun Thune, the wizard. The secrets of life and death are his, and the stars in the sky and the lands beneath the seas."

Kull looked at the girl. Fine gold was her hair and her violet eyes were slanted strangely; she was beautiful, but her beauty meant little to Kull.

"Tuzun Thune," he repeated. "Who is he?"

"A wizard of the Elder Race. He lives here in Valusia, by the Lake of Visions in the House of a Thousand Mirrors. All things are known to him, lord king; he speaks with the dead and holds converse with the demons of the Lost Lands."

Kull arose.

"I will seek out this mummer; but no word of my going, do you hear?"

"I am your slave, my lord." And she sank to her knees meekly, but the smile of her scarlet mouth was cunning behind Kull's back and the gleam of her narrow eyes was crafty.

Kull came to the house of Tuzun Thune, beside the Lake of Visions. Wide and blue stretched the waters of the lake, and many a fine palace rose upon its banks; many swan-winged pleasure boats drifted lazily upon its hazy surface and evermore there came the sound of soft music.

Tall and spacious, but unpretentious, rose the House of a Thousand Mirrors. The great doors stood open, and Kull ascended the broad stair and entered, unannounced. There in a great chamber, whose walls were of mirrors, he came upon Tuzun Thune, the wizard. The man was ancient as the hills of Zalgara; like wrinkled leather was his skin, but his cold gray eyes were like sparks of sword steel.

"Kull of Valusia, my house is yours," said he, bowing with old-time courtliness and motioning Kull to a throne-like chair.

"You are a wizard, I have heard," said Kull bluntly, resting his chin upon his hand and fixing his sombre eyes upon the man's face. "Can you do wonders?"

The wizard stretched forth his hand; his fingers opened and closed like a bird's claws.

"Is that not a wonder—that this blind flesh obeys the thoughts of my mind? I walk, I breathe, I speak—are they not all wonders?"

Kull meditated awhile, then spoke. "Can you summon up demons?"

"Aye. I can summon up a demon more savage than any in ghostland—by smiting you in the face."

Kull started, then nodded. "But the dead, can you talk to the dead?"

"I talk with the dead always—as I am talking now. Death begins with birth, and each man begins to die when he is born; even now you are dead, King Kull, because you were born."

"But you, you are older than men become; do wizards never die?"

"Men die when their times come. No later, no sooner. Mine has not come."

Kull turned these answers over in his mind.

"Then it would seem that the greatest wizard of Valusia is no more than an ordinary man, and I have been duped in coming here."

Tuzun Thune shook his head. "Men are but men, and

the greatest men are they who soonest learn the simpler things. Nay, look into my mirrors, Kull."

The ceiling was a great many mirrors, and the walls were mirrors, perfectly joined, yet many mirrors of many sizes and shapes.

"Mirrors are the world, Kull," droned the wizard. "Gaze into my mirrors and be wise."

Kull chose one at random and looked into it intently. The mirrors upon the opposite wall were reflected there, reflecting others, so that he seemed to be gazing down a long, luminous corridor, formed by mirror behind mirror; and far down this corridor moved a tiny figure. Kull looked long ere he saw that the figure was the reflection of himself. He gazed and a queer feeling of pettiness came over him; it seemed that that tiny figure was the true Kull, representing the real proportions of himself. So he moved away and stood before another.

"Look closely, Kull. That is the mirror of the past," he heard the wizard say.

Gray fogs obscured the vision, great billows of mist, ever heaving and changing like the ghost of a great river; through these fogs Kull caught swift fleeting visions of horror and strangeness; beasts and men moved there and shapes neither men nor beasts; great exotic blossoms glowed through the grayness; tall tropic trees towered high over reeking swamps, where reptilian monsters wallowed, and bellowed; the sky was ghastly with flying dragons, and the restless seas rocked and roared and beat endlessly along the muddy beaches. Man was not, yet man was the dream of the gods, and strange were the nightmare forms that glided through the noisome jungles. Battle and onslaught were there, and frightful love. Death was there, for Life and Death go hand in hand. Across the slimy beaches of the world sounded the bellowing of the monsters, and incredible shapes loomed through the streaming curtain of the incessant rain.

"This is of the future."

Kull looked in silence.

"See you—what?"

"A strange world," said Kull heavily. "The Seven Empires are crumbled to dust and are forgotten. The restless green waves roar for many a fathom above the eternal hills of Atlantis; the mountains of Lemuria of the West are the islands of an unknown sea. Strange savages roam the elder lands and new lands flung strangely from the deeps, defiling the elder shrines. Valusia is vanished and all the nations of today; they of tomorrow are strangers. They know us not."

"Time strides onward," said Tuzun Thune calmly. "We live today; what care we for tomorrow—or yesterday? The Wheel turns and nations rise and fall; the world changes, and times return to savagery to rise again through the long age. Ere Atlantis was, Valusia was, and ere Valusia was, the Elder Nations were. Aye, we, too, trampled the shoulders of lost tribes in our advance. You, who have come from the green sea hills of Atlantis to seize the ancient crown of Valusia, you think my tribe is old, we who held these lands ere the Valusians came out of the East, in the days before there were men in the sea lands. But men were here when the Elder Tribes rode out of the waste lands, and men before men, tribe before tribe. The nations pass and are forgotten, for that is the destiny of man."

"Yes," said Kull. "Yet is it not a pity that the beauty and glory of men should fade like smoke on a summer sea?"

"For what reason, since that is their destiny? I brood not over the lost glories of my race, nor do I labor for races to come. Live now, Kull, live now. The dead are dead; the unborn are not. What matters men's forgetfulness of you when you have forgotten yourself in the silent worlds of death? Gaze in my mirrors and be wise."

Kull chose another mirror and gazed into it.

"That is the mirror of deepest magic; what see ye, Kull?"

"Naught but myself."

"Look closely, Kull; is it in truth you?"

Kull stared into the great mirror, and the image that was his reflection returned his gaze.

"I come before this mirror," mused Kull, chin on fist, "and I bring this man to life. That is beyond my understanding, since first I saw him in the still waters of the lakes of Atlantis, till I saw him again in the gold-rimmed mirrors of Valusia. He is I, a shadow of myself, part of myself—I can bring him into being or slay him at my will; yet—" He halted, strange thoughts whispering through the vast dim recesses of his mind like shadowy bats flying through a great cavern—"yet where is he when I stand not in front of a mirror? May it be in man's power thus lightly to form and destroy a shadow of life and existence? How do I know that when I step back from the mirror he vanishes into the void of Naught?

"Nay, by Valka, am I the man or is he? Which of us is the ghost of the other? Mayhap these mirrors are but windows through which we look into another world. Does he think the same of me? Am I no more than a shadow, a reflection of himself—to him, as he to me? And if I am the ghost, what sort of a world lives upon the other side of this mirror? What armies ride there and what kings rule? This world is all I know. Knowing naught of any other, how can I judge? Surely there are green hills there and booming seas and wide plains where men ride to battle. Tell me, wizard who is wiser than most men, tell me are there worlds beyond our worlds?"

"A man has eyes, let him see," answered the wizard. "Who would see must first believe."

The hours drifted by, and Kull still sat before the mirrors of Tuzun Thune, gazing into that which depicted himself. Sometimes it seemed that he gazed upon hard shallowness; at other times gigantic depths seemed to loom before him. Like the surface of the sea was the mirror of Tuzun Thune; hard as the sea in the sun's slanting beams, in the darkness of the stars, when no eye can pierce her deeps; vast and mystic as the sea when the sun smites her in such way that the watcher's breath is caught at the glimpse of tremendous abysses. So was the mirror in which Kull gazed.

At last the king rose with a sigh and took his departure still wondering. And Kull came again to the House of a Thousand Mirrors; day after day he came and sat for hours before the mirror. The eyes looked out at him, identical with his; yet Kull seemed to sense a difference—a reality that was not of him. Hour upon hour he would stare with strange intensity into the mirror; hour after hour the image gave back his gaze.

The business of the palace and of the council went neglected. The people murmured; Kull's stallion stamped restlessly in his stable, and Kull's warriors diced and argued aimlessly with one another. Kull heeded not. At times he seemed on the point of discovering some vast, unthinkable secret. He no longer thought of the image in the mirror as a shadow of himself; the thing, to him, was an entity, similar in outer appearance, yet basically as far from Kull himself as the poles are far apart. The image, it seemed to Kull, had an individuality apart from Kull's, he was no more dependent on Kull than Kull was dependent on him. And day by day Kull doubted in which world he really lived; was he the shadow, summoned at will by the other? Did he instead of the other live in a world of delusion, the shadow of the real world?

Kull began to wish that he might enter the personality beyond the mirror for a space, to see what might be seen; yet should he manage to go beyond that door could he ever return? Would he find a world identical with the one in which he moved? A world, of which his was but a ghostly reflection? Which was reality and which illusion?

At times Kull halted to wonder how such thoughts and dreams had come to enter his mind, and at times he wondered if they came of his own volition or—here his thoughts would become mazed. His meditations were his own; no man ruled his thoughts, and he would summon them at his pleasure; yet could he? Were they not as bats, coming and going, not at his pleasure but at the bidding or ruling of—of whom? The gods? The Women who wove the webs of Fate? Kull could come to no conclusion, for at each mental step he became more and more bewildered in a hazy fog of illusory assertions and refutations. This much he knew; that strange visions entered his mind, like flying unbidden from the whispering void of nonexistence; never had he thought these thoughts, but now they ruled his mind, sleeping and waking, so that he seemed to walk in a daze at times; and his sleep was fraught with strange, monstrous dreams.

"Tell me, wizard," he said, sitting before the mirror, eyes fixed intently upon his image, "how can I pass yon door? For of a truth, I am not sure that that is the real world and this the shadow; at least, that which I see must exist in some form."

"See and believe," droned the wizard. "Man must believe to accomplish. Form is shadow, substance is illusion, materiality is dream; man is because he believes he is; what is man but a dream of the gods? Yet man can be that which he wishes to be; form and substance, they are but shadows. The mind, the ego, the essence of the god-dream—that is real, that is immortal. See and believe, if you would accomplish, Kull."

The king did not fully understand; he never fully understood the enigmatical utterances of the wizard; yet they struck somewhere in his being a dim responsive chord. So day after day he sat before the mirrors of Tuzun Thune. Ever the wizard lurked behind him like a shadow.

Then came a day when Kull seemed to catch glimpses of strange lands; there flitted across his consciousness dim thoughts and recognitions. Day by day he had seemed to lose touch with the world; all things had seemed each succeeding day more ghostly and unreal; only the man in the mirror seemed like reality. Now Kull seemed to be close to the doors of some mightier worlds; giant vistas gleamed fleetingly; the fogs of unreality thinned; "form is shadow, substance is illusion; they are but shadows" sounded as if from some far country of his consciousness. He remembered the wizard's words and it seemed to him that now he almost understood—form and substance, could not he change himself at will, if he knew the master key that opened this door? What worlds within what worlds awaited the bold explorer?

The man in the mirror seemed smiling at him—closer, closer—a fog enwrapped all and the reflection dimmed suddenly—Kull knew a sensation of fading, of change, of merging. . . .

"Kull!" the yell split the silence into a million vibratory fragments!

Mountains crashed and worlds tottered as Kull, hurled back by the frantic shout, made a superhuman effort, how or why he did not know.

A crash, and Kull stood in the room of Tuzun Thune before a shattered mirror, mazed and half-blind with bewilderment. There before him lay the body of Tuzun Thune, whose time had come at last, and above him stood Brule the Spear-slayer, sword dripping red and eyes wide with a kind of horror.

"Valka!" swore the warrior. "Kull, it was time I came!"

"Aye, yet what happened?" The king groped for words.

"Ask this traitress," answered the Spear-slayer, indicating a girl who crouched in terror before the king; Kull saw that it was she who first sent him to Tuzun Thune. "As I came in I saw you fading into yon mirror as smoke fades into the sky, by Valka! Had I not seen I would not have believed—you had almost vanished when my shout brought you back."

"Aye," muttered Kull, "I had almost gone beyond the door that time."

"This fiend wrought most craftily," said Brule. "Kull, do you not now see how he spun and flung over you a web of magic? Kaanuub of Blaal plotted with this wizard to do away with you, and this wench, a girl of the Elder Race, put the thought in your mind so that you would come here. Ka-nu of the council learned of the plot today; I know not what you saw in that mirror, but with it Tuzun Thune enthralled your soul and almost by his witchery he changed your body to mist—"

"Aye." Kull was still mazed. "But being a wizard, having knowledge of all the ages and despising gold, glory, and position, what could Kaanuub offer Tuzun Thune that would make of him a foul traitor?"

"Gold, power, and position," grunted Brule. "The sooner you learn that men are men whether wizard, king, or thrall, the better you will rule, Kull. Now what of her?"

"Naught, Brule," as the girl whimpered and groveled at Kull's feet. "She was but a tool. Rise, child, and go your ways; none shall harm you."

Alone with Brule, Kull looked for the last time on the mirrors of Tuzun Thune.

"Mayhap he plotted and conjured, Brule; nay, I doubt you not, yet—was it his witchery that was changing me to thin mist, or had I stumbled on a secret? Had you not brought me back, had I faded in dissolution or had I found worlds beyond this?"

Brule stole a glance at the mirrors, and twitched his shoulders as if he shuddered. "Aye, Tuzun Thune stored the wisdom of all the hells here. Let us be gone, Kull, ere they bewitch me, too."

"Let us go, then," answered Kull, and side by side they went forth from the House of a Thousand Mirrors—where, mayhap, are prisoned the souls of men.

None look now in the mirrors of Tuzun Thune. The pleasure boats shun the shore where stands the wizard's house, and no one goes in the house or to the room where Tuzun Thune's dried and withered carcass lies before the mirrors of illusion. The place is shunned as a place accursed, and though it stands for a thousand years to come, no footsteps shall echo there. Yet Kull upon his throne meditates often upon the strange wisdom and untold secrets hidden there and wonders. . . .

For there are worlds beyond worlds, as Kull knows, and whether the wizard bewitched him by words or by mesmerism, vistas did open to the king's gaze beyond that strange door, and Kull is less sure of reality since he gazed into the mirrors of Tuzun Thune.

THE KING AND THE OAK

Before the shadows slew the sun
    the kites were soaring free,
And Kull rode down the forest road,
    his red sword at his knee;
And winds were whispering round the world:
    "King Kull rides to the sea."

The sun dried crimson in the sea,
    the long gray shadows fell;
The moon rose like a silver skull
    that wrought a demon's spell,
For in its light great trees stood up
    like spectres out of hell.

In spectral light the trees stood up,
    inhuman monsters dim;
Kull thought each trunk a living shape,
    each branch a knotted limb,
And strange unmortal evil eyes flamed horribly at him.

The branches writhed like knotted snakes,
    they beat against the night,
And one gray oak with swayings stiff, horrific in his sight,
Tore up its roots and blocked his way,
    grim in the ghostly light.

165

They grappled in the forest way, the king and grisly oak;
Its great limbs bent him in their grip,
      but never a word was spoke;
And futile in his iron hand, the stabbing dagger broke.

And through the tossing, monstrous trees
      there sang a dim refrain
Fraught deep with twice a million years
      of evil, hate and pain:
"We were the lords ere man had come
      and shall be lords again."

Kull sensed an empire strange and old
      that bowed to man's advance
As kingdoms of the grass-blades before the marching ants,
And horror gripped him; in the dawn
      like someone in a trance.

He strove with bloody hands
      against a still and silent tree;
As from a nightmare dream he woke!
      a wind blew down the lea,
And Kull of high Atlantis rode silent to the sea.

THE BLACK CITY

(Fragment)

The cold eyes of Kull, king of Valusia, clouded with perplexity as they rested on the man who had so abruptly entered the royal presence and who now stood before the king, trembling with passion. Kull sighed; he knew the barbarians who served him, for was not he himself an Atlantean by birth? Brule, the Spear-slayer, bursting rudely into the king's chamber, had torn from his harness every emblem given him by Valusia and now stood bare of any sign to show that he was allied to the empire. And Kull knew the meaning of this gesture.

"Kull!" barked the Pict, pale with fury. "I will have justice!"

Again Kull sighed. There were times when peace and quiet were things to be desired and in Kamula he thought he had found them. Dreamy Kamula—even as he waited for the raging Pict to continue his tirade, Kull's thoughts drifted away and back along the lazy, dreamy days that had passed since his coming to this mountain city, this metropolis of pleasure, whose marble and lapis lazuli palaces were built, tier upon gleaming tier, about the dome-shaped hill that formed the city's center.

"My people have been allies of the empire for a thousand years!" The Pict made a swift, passionate gesture with his clenched fist. "Now, is it that one of my warriors can be snatched from under my nose in the very palace of the king?"

Kull straightened with a start.

"What madness is this? What warrior? Who seized him?"

"That's for you to discover," growled the Pict. "One moment he was there, lounging against a marble column—the next—zut! He was gone with only a foul stench and a frightful scream for clue."

"Perhaps a jealous husband—" mused Kull.

Brule broke in rudely: "Grogar never looked at any women—even of his own race. These Kamulians hate we Picts. I have read it in their looks."

Kull smiled. "You dream, Brule; these people are too indolent and pleasure-loving to hate anyone. They love, they sing, they compose lyrics—I suppose you think Grogar was snatched away by the poet Talligaro, or the singing woman Zareta, or prince Mandara?"

"I care not!" snarled Brule. "But I tell you this, Kull, Grogar has spilt his blood like water for the empire, and he is my best chief of mounted bowmen. I will find him, alive or dead, if I have to tear Kamula apart, stone by stone! By Valka, I will feed this city to the flames and quench the flames in blood—"

Kull had risen from his chair.

"Take me to the place you last saw Grogar," he said, and Brule ceased his tirade and led the way sullenly. They passed out of the chamber through an inner door and proceeded down a winding corridor, side by side, as different in appearance as two men could well be, yet alike in the litheness of movement, the keenness of eye, the intangible wildness that proclaimed the barbarian.

Kull was tall, broad-shouldered and deep-chested—massive yet lithe. His face was brown from sun and wind, his square-cut black hair like a lion's mane, his gray eyes cold as a sword gleaming through fathoms of ice.

Brule was typical of his race—of medium height, built

with the savage economy of a panther, and of skin much darker than the king's.

"We were in the Jeweled Room," grunted the Pict, "Grogar, Manaro and I. Grogar was leaning against a half-column set into the wall when he shifted his weight full against the wall—and vanished before our eyes! A panel swung inward and he was gone—and we had but a glimpse of black darkness within, and a loathsome scent flowed momentarily outward. But Manaro, standing beside Grogar, whipped out his sword in that instant and thrust the good blade into the opening, so the panel could not wholly close. We thrust against it, but it did not yield and I hastened after you, leaving Manaro holding his sword in the crack."

"And why did you tear off your Valusian emblems?" asked Kull.

"I was angry," growled the Spear-slayer sullenly, avoiding Kull's eye. The king nodded without reply. It was the natural, unreasoning action of an infuriated savage, to whom no natural enemy appears to be slashed and rent.

They entered the Jeweled Room, the further wall of which was set into the natural stone of the hill on which Kamula was built.

"Manaro swore he heard a whisper as of music," grunted Brule. "And there he leans with his ear at the crack. Hola—Manaro!"

Kull frowned as he saw the tall Valusian did not change his posture or give any heed to the hail. He did in truth lean against the panel, one hand gripping the sword which held the secret doorway apart, one ear glued to the thin crack. Kull noted the almost material darkness of that thin strip of blackness—it seemed to him that beyond that unknown opening, the darkness must lurk like a living, sentient thing.

He strode forward impatiently and clapped the soldier heavily on the shoulder. And Manaro rocked away from the wall and fell stiffly to lie at Kull's feet with horror-glazed eyes staring blankly upward.

"Valka!" swore Brule. "He's been stabbed—I was a fool to leave him here alone—"

The king shook his lionlike head. "There's no blood on him—look at his face." Brule looked and cursed. The dead Valusian's features were set in a mask of horror—and the effect was distinctly one of *listening*.

Kull cautiously approached the crack in the wall and then beckoned Brule. From somewhere beyond that mysterious portal sounded a thin, wailing sound as of a ghostly piping. It was so dim as to barely be heard, but it held in its music all the hate and venom of a thousand demons. Kull shrugged his giant shoulders.

UNTITLED

(Fragment)

"Thus," said Tu, chief councilor, "did Lala-ah, countess of Fanara, flee with her lover, Fenar, Farsunian adventurer, bringing shame to her husband-to-be and to the nation of Valusia."

Kull, fist supporting chin, nodded. He had listened with scant interest to the tale of how the young countess of Fanara had left a Valusian nobleman waiting on the steps of Merama's and had eloped with a man of her own choice.

"Yes," he impatiently interrupted Tu, "I understand. But what have the amorous adventures of a giddy girl to do with me? I blame her not for forsaking Ka-yanna— by Valka, he is as ugly as a rhinoceros and has a more abominable disposition. Then why tell me this tale?"

"You do not understand, Kull," said Tu, with the patience one must accord a barbarian who happens to be a king, besides. "The customs of the nation are not your customs. Lala-ah, by deserting Ka-yanna at the very foot of the altar where their nuptials were to be consummated, committed a very gross offense to the traditions of the land—and an insult to the nation is an insult to the king, Kull. For this alone she must be brought back and punished.

"Then, she is a countess, and it is a Valusian tradition that noble women marry foreigners only with the consent of the Valusian state—here consent was never given nor even asked. Valusia will become the scorn of all nations if we allow men from other lands to take our women with impunity."

"Name of Valka," grumbled Kull. "Here is a great to-do—custom and tradition! I have heard little else since I first pressed the throne of Valusia. In my land women mate with whom they will and with whom they choose."

"Aye, Kull," thus Tu, soothingly. "But this is Valusia—not Atlantis. There all men, aye, and all women, are free and unhindered, but civilization is a network and a maze of precedences and custom. And another thing in regard to the young countess: she has a strain of royal blood."

"This man rode with Ka-yanna's horsemen in pursuit of the girl," said Tu.

"Aye," the young man spoke, "and I have for you a word from Fenar, lord king."

"A word for me? I never saw Fenar."

"Nay, but this he said to a border guard of Zarfhaana, to be repeated to they who pursued: 'Tell the barbarian swine who defiles an ancient throne that I name him scoundrel. Tell him that some day I shall return and clothe his cowardly carcass in the clothing of women, to attend my chariot horses.'"

Kull's vast bulk heaved erect, his chair of state crashing to the floor. A moment he stood, speechless, then he found voice in a roar that sent Tu and the noble backward.

"Valka, Honen, Holgar, and Hotath!" he roared, mingling deities with heathen gods in a manner that made Tu's hair rise at the blasphemy. Kull's huge arms were brandished aloft and his mighty fist descended on the tabletop with a force that buckled the heavy legs like paper. Tu, pale, swept off his feet by this tide of barbarian fury, backed against the wall, followed by the young noble who had dared much in giving Fenar's word. However, Kull was too much the savage to connect the insult with the bearer; it must remain for civilized rulers to wreak vengeance on couriers.

"Horses!" roared Kull. "Have the Red Slayers mount! Send Brule to me!"

He tore off his kingly robe and hurled it across the room, snatched a costly vase from the broken table and dashed it to the floor.

"Hurry!" gasped Tu, shoving the young nobleman toward the door. "Get Brule, the Pictish Spear-slayer— haste, before he slays us all!"

Tu judged the king's actions by those of preceding kings; however, Kull had not progressed far enough in civilized custom to wreak his royal rage on innocent subjects.

His first red fury had been succeeded by a cold steel rage by the time Brule arrived. The Pict stalked in unconcernedly, a grim smile touching his lips as he marked the destruction caused by the king's wrath.

Kull was garbing himself in riding garments and he looked up as Brule entered, his scintillant gray eyes gleaming coldly.

"Kull, we ride?" asked the Pict.

"Aye, we ride hard and far, by Valka! We ride to Zarfhaana first and perhaps beyond—to the lands of the snow or the desert sands or to Hell! Have three hundred of the Red Slayers in readiness."

Brule grinned in pure enjoyment. He was a powerfully built man of medium height, with glittering eyes set in immobile features. He looked much like a bronze statue. Without a word he turned and left the chamber.

"Lord king, what do you do?" ventured Tu, still shaking from fright.

"I ride on Fenar's trail," answered the king ferociously. "The kingdom is in your hands, Tu. I return when I have crossed swords with this Farsunian or I do not return at all."

"Nay, nay!" exclaimed Tu. "This is most unwise, king! Heed not what that nameless adventurer said! The emperor of Zarfhaana will never allow you to bring such a force as you named into his realm."

"Then I will ride over the ruins of Zarfhaana's cities," was Kull's grim reply. "Men avenge their own insults in Atlantis—and though Atlantis has disowned and I am king of Valusia—still I am a man, by Valka!"

He buckled on his great sword and strode to the door, Tu staring after him.

There before the palace sat four hundred men in their saddles. Three hundred of these were men of the Red Slayers, Kull's cavalry, and the most terrible soldiery of the earth. They were composed mostly of Valusian hillmen, the strongest and most vigorous of a degenerating race. The remaining hundred were Picts, lean, powerful savages, men of Brule's tribe, who sat their horses like centaurs and fought like demons when occasion arose.

All these men gave Kull the crown salute as he strode down the palace steps and his eyes lighted with a fierce gleam. He was almost grateful to Fenar for having given him the pretext he needed to quit the monotonous life of the court for awhile and plunge into fierce action— but his thoughts toward the Farsunian were no more kindly for this reason.

At the front of this fierce array sat Brule, chieftain of Valusia's most formidable allies, and Kelkor, second commander of the Red Slayers.

Kull acknowledged the salute by a brusque gesture and swung into the saddle.

Brule and the commander reined in on either side of him.

"At attention," came Kelkor's curt command. "Spurs! Forward!"

The cavalcade moved forward at an easy trot. The people of Valusia gazed curiously from their windows and doorways, and the throngs on the streets turned as the clatter of silver hoofs resounded through the babble and chatter of trading and commerce. The steeds flung their caparisoned manes; the bronze armor of the warriors glinted in the sun, the pennons on the long lances streamed backward. A moment the small people of the marketplace stopped their gabble as the proud array swept by, blinking in stupid wonder or childish admiration; then the horsemen dwindled down the great white street, the clang of silver on cobblestone died away in the distance, and the people of the city turned back to their commonplace tasks. As the people always do, no matter what kings ride.

Along the broad white streets of Valusia swept the king and his horsemen, out through the suburbs with their spacious estates and lordly palaces; on and on until the golden spires and sapphire towers of Valusia were but a silver shimmer in the distance and the green hills of Zalgara loomed majestically before them.

Night found them encamped high on the slopes of the mountains. The hill people, kin to the Red Slayers, many of them, flocked to the camp with gifts of food and wine, and the warriors, the proud restraint they felt among the cities of the world loosened, talked with them and sang old songs, and exchanged old tales. But Kull walked apart, beyond the glow of the campfires, to gaze out across the mystic vistas of crag and valley. The slopes were softened by verdure and foliage, the vales deepening into shadowy realms of magic, the hills standing out bold and clear in the silver of the moon. The hills of Zalgara had always held a fascination for Kull. They brought to his mind the mountains of Atlantis whose snowy heights he had scaled as a youth, ere he fared forth into the great world to write his name across the stars and make an ancient throne his seat.

Yet there was a difference. The crags of Atlantis rose stark and gaunt; her cliffs were barren and rugged. The mountains of Atlantis were brutal and terrible with youth, even as Kull. Age had not softened their might. The hills of Zalgara rose up like ancient gods, but green groves and waving verdure laughed upon their shoulders and cliffs, and their outline was soft and flowing. Age—age— thought Kull; many a drifting century had worn away their craggy splendor; they were mellow and beautiful with antiquity. Ancient mountains dreaming of bygone kings whose careless feet had trod their sward.

Like a red wave the thought of Fenar's insult swept away these broodings. Hands clenched in fury, Kull flung back his shoulders to gaze full into the calm eye of the moon.

"Helfara and Hotath doom my soul to everlasting Hell if I wreak not my vengeance on Fenar!" he snarled.

The night breeze whispered among the trees as if in answer to the heathen vow.

Ere scarlet dawn had burst like a red rose over the hills of Zalgara Kull's cavalcade was in the saddle. The first glints of morning shone on the lance points, the helmets and the shields as the band wound its way through green-waving vales and up over long undulating slopes.

"We ride into the sunrise," remarked Kelkor.

"Aye," was Brule's grim response. "And some of us ride beyond the sunrise."

Kelkor shrugged his shoulders. "So be it. That is the destiny of a warrior."

Kull glanced at the commander. Straight as a spear sat Kelkor in his saddle, inflexible, unbending as a statue of steel. The commander had always reminded the king of a fine sword of polished steel. A man of terrific power and mighty forces, the most powerful thing about him was his absolute control of himself. An icy calmness had always characterized his words and deeds. In the heat and vituperation of council, in the wild wrack of battle, Kelkor was always cool, never confused. He had few friends, nor did he strive to make friends. His qualities alone had raised him from an unknown warrior in the ranks of the mercenaries to the second highest rank in Valusian armies—and only the fact of his birth debarred him from the highest. For custom decreed that the lord commander of troops must be a Valusian and Kelkor was a Lemurian. Yet he looked more a Valusian than a Lemurian as he sat his horse, for he was built differently from most of his race, being tall and leanly but strongly built. His strange eyes alone betrayed his race.

Another dawn found them riding down from the foothills that debauched out into the Camoonian desert, a vast wasteland, uninhabited, a dreary waste of yellow sands. No trees grew there, nor even bushes, nor were there any streams of water. All day they rode, stopping only a short time at midday to eat and rest the horses, though the heat was almost intolerable. The men, inured as they were, wilted beneath the heat. Silence reigned save for the clank of stirrups and armor, the creak of sweating saddles, and the monotonous scruff of hoof through the deep sands. Even Brule hung his corselet on his saddlebow. But Kelkor sat upright and unmoved, under the weight of full armor, seemingly untouched by the heat and discomfort that harried the rest.

"Steel, all steel," thought Kull in admiration, secretly wondering if he could ever attain the perfect mastery over himself that this man, also a barbarian, had attained.

Two days' journey brought them out of the desert and into the low hills that marked the confines of Zarfhaana. At the borderline they were stopped by two Zarfhaanian riders.

"I am Kull of Valusia," the king answered abruptly. "I ride on the trail of Fenar. Seek not to hinder my passing. I will be responsible to your emperor."

The two horsemen reined aside to let the cavalcade pass and as the clashing hoofs faded in the distance, one spoke to the other.

"I win our wager. The king of Valusia rides himself."

"Aye," the other replied. "These barbarians avenge their own wrongs. Had the king been a Valusian, by Valka, you had lost."

The vales of Zarfhaana echoed to the tramp of Kull's

riders. The peaceful country people flocked out of their villages to watch the fierce warriors sweep by, and word went to the north and the south, the west and the east, that Kull of Valusia rode eastward.

Just beyond the frontier, Kull, having sent an envoy to the Zarfhaanian emperor to assure him of their peaceful intention, held council with Brule, Ka-yanna, and Kelkor.

"They have the start of us by many days," said Kull, "and we must lose no time in searching for their trail. These country people will lie to us; we must scent out our own trail, as wolves scent out the spoor of a deer."

"Let me question these fellows," said Ka-yanna, with a vicious curl of his thick, sensual lips. "I will guarantee to make them speak truthfully."

Kull glanced at him inquiringly.

"There are ways," purred the Valusian.

"Torture?" grunted Kull, his lip writhing in unveiled contempt. "Zarfhaana is a friendly nation."

"What cares the emperor for a few wretched villagers?" blandly asked Ka-yanna.

"Enough." Kull swept aside the suggestion with true Atlantean abhorrence, but Brule raised his hand for attention.

"Kull," said he, "I like this fellow's plan no more than you, but at times even a swine speaks truth." Ka-yanna's lips writhed in rage, but the Pict gave him no heed. "Let me take a few of my men among the villagers and question them. I will only frighten a few, harming no one; otherwise we may spend weeks in futile search."

"There spake the barbarian," said Kull with the friendly maliciousness that existed between the two.

"In what city of the Seven Empires were you born, lord king?" asked the Pict with sarcastic deference.

Kelkor dismissed this byplay with an impatient wave of his hand.

"Here is our position," said he, scrawling a map in the ashes of the campfire with his scabbard end. "North Fenar is not likely to go—assuming as we do that he does not intend remaining in Zarfhaana—because beyond Zarfhaana is the sea, swarming with pirates and sea-rovers. South he will not go because there lies Thurania, foe of his nation. Now it is my guess that he will strike straight east as he was traveling, cross Zarfhaana's eastern border somewhere near the frontier city of Talunia, and go into the wastelands of Grondar; thence I believe he will turn south seeking to gain Farsun— which lies west of Valusia—through the small principalities south of Thurania."

"Here is much supposition, Kelkor," said Kull. "If Fenar wishes to win through to Farsun, why in Valka's name did he strike in the exactly opposite direction?"

"Because, as you know, Kull, in these unsettled times all our borders, except the easternmost, are closely guarded. He could never have gotten through without proper explanation, much less have carried the countess with him."

"I believe Kelkor is right, Kull," said Brule, eyes dancing with impatience to be in the saddle. "His arguments sound logical at any rate."

"As good a plan as any," replied Kull. "We ride east."

And east they rode through the long lazy days, entertained and feasted at every halt by the kindly Zarfhaanian people. A soft and lazy land, thought Kull, a dainty girl waiting helplessly for some ruthless conqueror—Kull dreamed his dreams as his riders' hoofs beat out their tattoo through the dreamy valleys and the verdant woodlands. Yet he drove his men hard, giving them no rest, for ever behind his far-sweeping and imperial visions of blood-stained glory and wild conquest, there loomed the phantom of his hate, the relentless hatred of the savage, before which all other desires must give way.

They swung wide of cities and large towns for Kull wished not to give his fierce warriors opportunity to become embroiled in some dispute with the inhabitants. The cavalcade was nearing the border city of Talunia, Zarfhaana's last eastern outpost, when the envoy sent to the emperor in his city to the north rejoined them with the word that the emperor was quite willing that Kull should ride through his land, and requested the Valusian king to visit him on his return. Kull smiled grimly at the irony of the situation, considering the fact that even while the emperor was giving benevolent permission, Kull was already far into his country with his men.

Kull's warriors rode into Talunia at dawn, after an all night's ride, for he had thought that perhaps Fenar and the countess, feeling temporarily safe, would tarry awhile in the border city and he wished to precede the word of his coming.

Kull encamped his men some distance outside the city walls and entered the city alone save for Brule. The gates were readily opened to him when he had shown the regal signet of Valusia and the symbol sent him by the Zarfhaanian emperor.

"Hark ye," said Kull to the commander of the gate guards, "are Fenar and Lala-ah in this city?"

"That I cannot say," the soldier answered. "They entered at this gate many days since, but whether they are still in the city or not, I do not know."

"Listen, then," said Kull, slipping a gemmed bracelet from his mighty arm, "I am merely a wandering Valusian noble, accompanied by a Pictish companion. None need know who I am, understand?"

The soldier eyed the costly ornament covetously. "Very good, lord king, but what of your soldiers encamped in the forest?"

"They are concealed from the eyes of the city. If any peasant enters your gate, question him and if he tells you of a force encamped, hold him prisoner for some trumped-up reason, until this time tomorrow. For by then I shall have secured the information I desire."

"Valka's name, lord king, you would make me a traitor of sorts!" expostulated the soldier. "I think not that you plan treachery, yet—"

Kull changed his tactics. "Have you not orders to obey

your emperor's command? Have I not shown you his symbol of command? Dare you disobey? Valka, it is you who would be the traitor!"

After all, reflected the soldier, this was the truth—he would not be bribed, no! no! But since it was the order of a king who bore authority from his emperor—

Kull handed over the bracelet with no more than a faint smile betraying his contempt of mankind's way of lulling their consciences into the path of their desires, refusing to admit that they violated their own moral senses, even to themselves.

The king and Brule walked through the streets, where the tradespeople were just beginning to stir. Kull's giant stature and Brule's bronze skin drew many curious stares, but no more than would be expected to be accorded strangers. Kull began to wish he had brought Kelkor or a Valusian, for Brule could not possibly disguise his race, and since Picts were seldom seen in these eastern cities, it might cause comment that would reach the hearing of those they sought.

They sought a modest tavern where they secured a room, then took their seats in the drinking room, to see if they might hear aught of what they wished to hear. But the day wore on and nothing was said of the fugitive couple, nor did carefully veiled questions elicit any knowledge. If Fenar and Lala-ah were still in Talunia they were certainly not advertising their presence. Kull would have thought that the presence of a dashing gallant and a beautiful young girl of royal blood in the city would have been the subject of at least some comment, but such seemed not to be the case.

Kull intended to fare forth that night upon the streets, even to the extent of committing some marauding if necessary, and failing in this to reveal his identity to the lord of the city the next morning, demanding that the culprits be handed over to him. Yet Kull's ferocious pride rebelled at such an act. This seemed the most logical course, and was one which Kull would have followed had the matter been merely a diplomatic or political one. But Kull's fierce pride was roused and he was loath to ask aid from anyone in the consummating of his vengeance.

Night was falling as the comrades stepped into the streets, still thronged with voluble people and lighted by torches set along the streets. They were passing a shadowy side-street when a cautious voice halted them. From the dimness between the great building a claw-like hand beckoned. With a swift · glance at each other, they stepped forward, warily loosening their daggers in their sheaths as they did so.

An aged crone, ragged, stooped with age, stole from the shadows.

"Aye, King Kull, what seek ye in Talunia?" Her voice was a shrill whisper.

"Kull's fingers closed about his dagger hilt more firmly as he replied guardedly.

"How know you my name?"

"The marketplaces speak and hear," she answered with a low cackle of unhallowed mirth. "A man saw and recognized you today in the tavern and the word has gone from mouth to mouth."

Kull cursed softly.

"Hark ye!" hissed the woman. "I can lead ye to those ye seek—if ye be willing to pay the price."

"I will fill your apron with gold," Kull answered swiftly.

"Good. Listen now. Fenar and the countess are apprised of your arrival. Even now they are preparing their escape. They have hidden in a certain house since early evening when they learned that you had come, and soon they leave their hiding place—"

"How can they leave the city?" interrupted Kull. "The gates are shut at sunset."

"Horses await them at a postern gate in the eastern wall. The guard has been bribed. Fenar has many friends in Talunia."

"Where hide they now?"

The crone stretched forth a shrivelled hand. "A token of good faith, lord king," she wheedled.

Kull put a coin in her hand and she smirked and made a grotesque curtsey.

"Follow me, lord king," and she hobbled away swiftly into the shadows.

The king and his companion followed her uncertainly through narrow, winding streets until she halted before an unlit huge building in a squalid part of the city.

"They hide in a room at the head of the stairs leading from the lower chamber opening into the street, lord king."

"How do you know that they do?" asked Kull suspiciously. "Why should they pick such a wretched place in which to hide?"

The woman laughed silently, rocking to and fro in her uncanny mirth.

"As soon as I made sure you were in Talunia, lord king, I hurried to the mansion where they had their abode and told them, offering to lead them to a place of concealment! Ho, ho, ho! They paid me good gold coins!"

Kull stared at her silently.

"Now, by Valka," said he, "I knew not civilization could produce a thing like this woman. Here, female, guide Brule to the gate where await the horses. Brule, go with her there and await my coming—perchance Fenar might give me the slip here—"

"But Kull," protested Brule, "you go not into yon dark house alone—bethink you this might all be an ambush!"

"This woman dare not betray me!" And the crone shuddered at the grim response. "Haste ye!"

As the two forms melted into the darkness, Kull entered the house. Groping with his hands until his feline-gifted eyes became accustomed to the total darkness, he found the stair and ascended it, dagger in hand, walking stealthily and on the lookout for creaking steps. For all his size, the king moved as easily and silently as a leopard, and had the watcher at the head of the stairs been awake, it is doubtful if he would have heard his coming.

As it was, he awakened when Kull's hand was clapped over his mouth, only to fall back temporarily unconscious as Kull's fist found his jaw.

The king crouched a moment above his victim, straining his faculties for any sound that might betoken that he had been heard. Utter silence reigned. He stole to the door. Ah, his keen senses detected a low confused mumble as of people whispering—a guarded movement—with one leap Kull hurled the door open and hurled himself into the room. He halted not to weigh chances; there might have been a roomful of assassins waiting for him for all he thought of the thing.

Everything then happened in an instant. Kull saw a barren room, lighted by moonlight that streamed in at the window, he caught a glimpse of two forms clambering through this window, one apparently carrying the other, a fleeting glance of a pair of dark, daring eyes in a face of piquant beauty, another laughing, reckless handsome face—all this he saw confusedly as he cleared the whole room with a tigerish bound, a roar of pure bestial ferocity breaking from his lips at the sight of his foe escaping. The window was empty even as he hurled across the sill, and raging and furious, he caught another glimpse, two forms darting into the shadows of a nearby maze of buildings—a silvery mocking laugh floated back to him, another stronger, more mocking. Kull flung a leg over the sill and dropped the sheer thirty feet to the earth disdaining the rope ladder that still swung from the window. He could not hope to follow them through that maze of streets, which they doubtless knew much better than he.

Sure of their destination, however, he raced toward the gate in the eastern wall, which from the crone's description was not far distant. However, some time elapsed before he arrived and when he did it was only to find Brule and the hag there.

"Nay," said Brule. "The horses are here, but none has come for them."

Kull cursed savagely. Fenar had tricked him after all, and the woman also. Suspecting treachery, the horses at that gate had only served as a blind. Fenar was doubtless escaping through some other gate, then.

"Swift!" shouted Kull. "Haste to the camp and have the men mount! I follow Fenar's trail."

And leaping upon one of the horses he was gone. Brule mounted the other and rode toward the camp. The crone watched them go, shaking with unholy mirth. After awhile she heard the drum of many hoofs passing the city.

"Ho, ho, ho! They ride into the sunrise—and who rides back from beyond the sunrise?"

All night Kull rode, striving to cut down the lead the Farsunian and the girl had gained. He knew they dared not remain in Zarfhaana and as the sea lay to the north, and Thurania, Farsun's ancient enemy, to the south, then there lay but one course for them—the road to Grondar.

The stars were paling when the ramparts of the eastern hills rose starkly against the sky in front of the king, and dawn was stealing over the grasslands as Kull's weary steed toiled up the pass and halted a moment at the summit. Here the fugitives must have passed for these cliffs stretched the whole length of the Zarfhaanian border and the next nearest pass was many a mile to the north. The Zarfhaanian in the small tower that reared up in the pass hailed the king, but Kull replied with a gesture and rode on.

At the crest of the pass he halted. There beyond lay Grondar. The cliffs rose as abruptly on the eastern side as they did upon the west and from their feet the grasslands stretched away endlessly. Mile upon countless mile of tall waving savannah land met his eyes, seemingly inhabited only by the herds of buffalo and deer that roamed those wild expanses. The east was fast reddening and as Kull sat his horse the sun flamed up over the savannahs like a wild blaze of fire, making it appear to the king as if all the grasslands were ablaze—limning the motionless horseman against its flame, so that man and horse seemed a single dark statue against the red morning to the riders who were just entering the first defile of the pass far behind. Then he vanished from their gaze as he spurred forward.

"He rides into the sunrise," muttered the warriors.

"Who rides back from the sunrise?"

The sun was high in the sky when the troop overtook Kull, the king having stopped to consult with his companions.

"Have your Picts spread out," said Kull. "Fenar and the countess will try to turn south any time now, for no man cares to ride any further into Grondar than need be. They might even seek to get past us and win back into Zarfhaana."

So they rode in open formation, Brule's Picts ranging like lean wolves far afield to the north and the south.

But the fugitives' trail led straight onward, Kull's trained eyes easily following the course through the tall grass, marking where the grass had been trampled and beaten down by the horses' hoofs. Evidently the countess and her lover rode alone.

And on into the wild country of Grondar they rode, pursuers and pursued.

How Fenar managed to keep that lead, Kull could not understand, but the soldiers were forced to spare their horses, while Fenar had extra steeds and could change from one to another, thus keeping each comparatively fresh.

Kull had sent no envoy to the king of Grondar. The Grondarians were a wild, half-civilized race, of whom little was known by the rest of the world, save that their raiding parties sometimes swept out of the grasslands to sweep the borders of Thurania and the lesser nations with torch and sword. Westward, their borders were plainly marked, clearly defined and carefully guarded, that is by their neighbors, but how far easterly their kingdom extended no one knew. It was vaguely supposed that their country extended to, and possibly included that vast expanse of untenable wilderness spoken of in myth and legend as The World's End.

Several days of hard riding had passed with neither sight of the fugitives nor any other human, when a Pictish rider sighted a band of horsemen approaching from the south.

Kull halted his force and waited. They rode up and halted at a distance, a band of some four hundred Grondarian warriors, fierce, leanly-built men, clad in leather garments and rude armor.

Their leader rode forth. "Stranger, what do ye in this land?"

Kull answered, "We pursue a disobedient subject and her lover, and we ride in peace. We have no dispute with Grondar."

The Grondarian sneered. "Men who ride in Grondar carry their lives in their right hands, stranger."

"Then, by Valka," roared Kull, losing patience, "my right hand is stronger to defend than all Grondar is to assail! Stand aside ere we trample you!"

"Lances at rest!" came Kelkor's curt voice; the forest of spears lowered as one, the warriors leaning forward.

The Grondarians gave back before that formidable array, unable, as they knew, to stand in the open the charge of fully armed horsemen. They reined aside, sitting their horses sullenly as the Valusians swept by them. The leader shouted after them.

"Ride on, fools! Who ride beyond the sunrise— return not!"

They rode, and though bands of horsemen circled their tracks at a distance like hawks, and they kept a heavy guard at night, the riders came not nearer nor were the outriders molested in any way.

The grasslands continued with never a hill or forest to break their monotony. Sometimes they came upon the almost obliterated ruins of some ancient city, mute reminders of the bloody days when, ages and ages since, the ancestors of the Grondarians had appeared from nowhere in particular and had conquered the original inhabitants of the land. They sighted no inhabited cities, none of the rough habitations of the Grondarians, for their way led through an especially wild, unfrequented part of the land. It became evident that Fenar intended not to turn back; his trail led straight east and whether he hoped to find sanctuary somewhere in that nameless land or whether he was seeking merely to tire his pursuers out, could not be said.

Long days of riding and then they came to a great river meandering through the plain. At its banks the grasslands came to an abrupt halt, and beyond, on the further side, a barren desert stretched to the horizon.

An ancient man stood upon the bank and a large, flat boat floated on the sullen surface of the water. The man was aged, but mightily built, as huge as Kull himself. He was clad only in ragged garments, seemingly as ancient as himself, but there was something kingly and awe-inspiring about the man. His snowy hair fell to his shoulders and his huge white beard, wild and unkempt, came almost to his waist. From beneath white, lowering brows, great luminous eyes blazed, undimmed by age.

"Stranger, who have the bearing of a king," said he to Kull in a great deep resonant voice, "would ye cross the river?"

"Aye," said Kull, "if they we seek crossed."

"A man and a girl rode my ferry yesterday at dawn," was the answer.

"Name of Valka!" swore Kull. "I could find it in me to admire the fool's courage! What city lies beyond this river, ferryman?"

"No city lies beyond," said the Elder man. "This river marks the border of Grondar—and the world!"

"How!" ejaculated Kull. "Have we ridden so far? I had thought that the desert which is the end of the world was part of Grondar's realm."

"Nay. Grondar ends here. Here is the end of the world; beyond is magic and the unknown. Here is the boundary of the world; there begins the realm of horror and mysticism. This is the river Stagus and I am Karon the Ferryman."

Kull looked at him in wonder, little knowing that he gazed upon one who should go down the dim centuries until myth and legend had changed the truth and Karon the Ferryman had become the boat-man of Hades.

"You are very aged," said Kull curiously, while the Valusians looked on the man with wonder and the savage Picts in superstitious awe.

"Aye. I am a man of the Elder Race, who ruled the world before Valusia was, or Grondar or Zarfhaana, riders from the sunset. Ye would cross this river? Many a warrior, many a king, have I ferried across. Remember, they who ride beyond the sunrise, return not! For of all the thousands who have crossed the Stagus, not one has returned. Three hundred years have passed since first I saw the light, king of Valusia. I ferried the army of King Gaar the Conqueror when he rode into World's End with all his mighty hosts. Seven days they were passing over, yet no man of them came back. Aye, the sound of battle and the clash of swords clanged out over the wastelands for a long while from sun to sun, but when the moon shone all was silence. Mark this, Kull, no man has ever returned from beyond the Stagus. Nameless horrors lurk in yonder lands and terrible are the ghastly shapes of doom I glimpse beyond the river in the vagueness of dusk and the grey of early dawn. Mark ye, Kull."

Kull turned in his saddle and eyed his men.

"Here my commands cease," said he. "As for myself, I ride on Fenar's trail if it lead to hell and beyond. Yet I bid no man follow beyond this river. Ye all have my permission to return to Valusia, nor shall any word of blame ever be spoken of you."

Brule reined to Kull's side.

"I ride with the king," he said curtly, and his Picts raised an acquiescing shout. Kelkor rode forward.

"They who would return, take a single pace forward," said he.

The metal ranks sat motionless as statues.

"They ride, Kull," grinned Brule.

A fierce pride rose in the king's savage soul. He spoke a single sentence, a sentence which thrilled his warriors more than an accolade.

"Ye are men."

Karon ferried them across, rowing over and returning until the entire force stood on the eastern bank. And though the boat was heavy and the ancient man rowed alone, yet his clumsy oars drove the unwieldy craft swiftly through the water and at the last journey he was no more weary than at the start.

Kull spake. "Since the desert throngs with wild things, how is it that none come into the lands of men?"

Karon pointed to the river, and looking closely Kull saw that the river swarmed with serpents and small fresh-water sharks.

"No man swims this river," said the ferryman. "Neither man nor mammoth."

"Forward," said Kull. "Forward; we ride. The land is free before us."

UNTITLED

(Fragment)

Three men sat at a table playing a game. Across the
sill of an open window there whispered a faint breeze,
blowing the filmy curtains about and bearing to the play-
ers the incense of roses and vines and growing green
things.

Three men sat at a table—one was a king—one a
prince of an ancient house—one was the chief of a terrible and barbaric nation.

"Score!" quoth Kull, king of Valusia, as he moved one
of the ivory figures. "My wizard menaces your warrior,
Brule."

Brule nodded. He was not as large a man as the king,
but he was firmly knit, compactly yet lithely built. Kull
was the tiger, Brule was the leopard. Brule was a Pict
and dark like all his race. Immobile features set off a
fine head, powerful neck, heavy trim shoulders and a
deep chest. These features, with the muscular legs and
arms, were characteristics of the nation to which he
belonged. But in one respect Brule differed from his
tribesmen, for whereas their eyes were mostly hard scintillant brown or wicked black, his were a deep volcanic
blue. Somewhere in his blood was a vagrant strain of

191

Celt or of those scattered savages who lived in ice caves close to the Arctic Circle.

"A wizard is a hard man to beat, Kull," said this man, "in this game or in the real game of battle—well, there was once when my life hung on the balance of power between a Pictland wizard and me—he had his charms and I had a well-forged blade—"

He paused to drink deeply from a crimson goblet which stood at his elbow.

"Tell us the tale, Brule," urged the third player. Ronaro, prince of the great Atl Volante house, was a slim elegant young man with a splendid head, fine dark eyes and a keen intellectual face. He was the patrician—the highest type of intelligent aristocracy any land has ever produced. These other two in a way were his antithesis. He was born in a palace; of the others, one had been born in a wattle hut, the other in a cave. Ronaro traced his descent back two thousand years, through a line of dukes, knights, princes, statesmen, poets, and kings. Brule could trace his ancestors vaguely for a few hundred years and he named among them skin-clad chiefs, painted and feathered warriors, shamans with bison-skull masks and finger-bone necklaces—one or two island kings who held court in mud huts, and a legendary hero or two, semi-deified for feats of personal strength or wholesale murder. Kull did not know who his own parents were.

But in the countenance of all three gleamed an equality beyond the shackles of birth and circumstance—the aristocracy of the Man. These men were natural patricians, each in his own way. Ronaro's ancestors were kings; Brule's, skin-clad chiefs; Kull's might have been slaves or chieftains. But about each of the three was that indefinable element which sets the superior man apart and shatters the delusion that all men were born equal.

"Well," Brule's eyes filled with brooding reminiscence, "it happened in my early youth; yes, in my first war raid. Oh, I had killed a man or so in the fishing brawls and at the tribal feasts, but I had not yet been ornamented with the scars of the warrior clan—" he indicated his bare breast where the listeners saw three small horizontal marks, barely discernible in the sun-bronze of the Pict's mighty chest.

Ronaro watched him with a never-failing interest as he talked. These fierce barbarians with their primitive vitality and straight-forwardness intrigued the young prince. Years in Valusia as one of the empire's strongest allies had wrought an outward change on the Pict—had not tamed him, but had given him a veneer of culture, education and reserve. But beneath that veneer burned the blind black savage of old. To a greater extent had this change worked on Kull, once warrior of Atlantis, now king of Valusia.

"You, Kull, and you, Ronaro," Brule said, "we of The Islands are all one blood, but of many tribes, and each tribe has customs and traditions peculiar to itself alone. We all acknowledge Nial of the Tatheli as over-king, but his rule is loose. He does not interfere with our affairs among ourselves, nor does he levy tribute or taxes, as the Valusians call it, from any except the Nargi and the Dano and the Whale-slayers who live on the isle of Tathel with his own tribe. These he protects against other tribes and for that reason he collects toll. But he takes no toll of my tribe, the Borni, nor of any other tribe. Neither does he interfere when two tribes go to war— unless some tribe encroaches on the three who pay tribute. When the war is fought and won, he arbitrates the matter, and his judgement is final—what stolen women shall be returned, what payment of war canoes made, what blood price paid, and so on. And when the Lemurians or the Celts or any foreign nation or band of reavers come against us, he sends forth for all tribes to put aside their quarrels and fight side by side. Which is a good thing. He might be a supreme tyrant if he liked, for his own tribe is very strong, and with the aid of Valusia he might do as he liked—but he knows that though he might, with his tribes and their allies, crush all the other tribes, there would never be peace again, but revolt as long as a Borni or a Sungara or a Wolf-slayer or any of the tribesmen was left alive."

THE CURSE OF THE GOLDEN SKULL

Rotath of Lemuria lay dying. Blood had ceased to flow from the deep sword gash under his heart, but the pulse in his temple hammered like kettledrums.

Rotath lay on a marble floor. Granite columns rose about him and a silver idol stared with ruby eyes at the man who lay at its feet. The bases of the columns were carved with curious monsters; above the shrine sounded a vague whispering. The trees which hemmed in and hid that mysterious fane spread long waving branches above it, and these branches were vibrant with leaves that rustled in the wind. From time to time, great black roses scattered their dusky petals down.

Rotath lay dying and he used his fading breath in calling down curses on his slayers—on the faithless king who had betrayed him, and on that barbarian chief, Kull of Atlantis, who dealt him the death blow.

Acolyte of the nameless gods, and dying in an unknown shrine on the leafy summit of Lemuria's highest mountain—Rotath's eyes smouldered with a terrible cold fire. A pageant of glory and splendor passed before his mind's eye. The acclaim of worshippers, the roar of silver trumpets, the whispering shadows of mighty and mystic temples where great wings swept unseen—then the intrigues, the onslaught of the invaders—death!

Rotath cursed the king of Lemuria—the king to whom

he had taught fearful and ancient mysteries and forgotten abominations. Fool that he had been to reveal his powers to a weakling, who, having learned to fear him, had turned to foreign kings for aid.

How strange it seemed, that he, Rotath of the Moon-stone and the Asphodel, sorcerer and magician, should be gasping out his breath on the marble floor, a victim to that most material of all threats—a keen pointed sword in a sinewy hand.

Rotath cursed the limitations of the flesh. He felt his brain crumbling and he cursed all the men of all the worlds. He cursed them by Hotath and Helgor, by Ra and Ka, and Valka.

He cursed all men living and dead, and all the generations unborn for a million centuries to come, naming Vramma and Jaggta-noga and Kamma and Kulthas. He cursed humanity by the fane of the Black Gods, the tracks of the Serpent Ones, the talons of the Ape Lords, and the iron-bound books of Shuma Gorath.

He cursed goodness and virtue and light, speaking the names of gods forgotten even by the priests of Lemuria. He invoked the dark monstrous shadows of the elder worlds, and of those black suns which lurk forever behind the stars.

He felt the shades gather about him. He was going fast. And closing about him in an ever nearing ring, he sensed the tiger-taloned devils who awaited his coming. He saw their bodies of solid jet and the great red caverns of their eyes. Behind hovered the white shadows of they who had died upon his altars, in horrid torment. Like mist in the moonlight they floated, great luminous eyes fixed on him in sad accusation, a never ending host.

Rotath feared, and fearing, his curses rose louder, his blasphemies grew more terrible. With one last wild passion of fury, he placed a curse on his own bones, that they might bring death and horror to the sons of men.

But even as he spoke, he knew that years and ages would pass and his bones turn to dust in that forgotten shrine before any man's foot disturbed its silence. So he mustered his fast waning powers for one last invocation to the dread beings he had served, one last feat of magic. He uttered a blood-freezing formula, naming a terrible name.

And soon he felt mighty elemental powers set in motion. He felt his bones growing hard and brittle. A coldness transcending earthly coldness passed over him and he lay still. The leaves whispered and the silver god laughed with cold gemmed eyes.

Years stretched into centuries, centuries became ages. The green oceans rose and wrote an epic poem in emerald and the rhythm thereof was terrible. Thrones toppled and the silver trumpets fell silent forever. The races of men passed as smoke drifts from the breast of a summer. The roaring jade green seas engulfed the lands and all mountains sank, even the highest mountain of Lemuria.

A man thrust aside the trailing vines and stared. A heavy beard masked his face and mire slimed his boots. Above and about him hung the thick tropic jungle in breathless and exotic brooding. Orchids flamed and breathed about him.

Wonder was in his wide eyes. He gazed between shattered granite columns upon a crumbling marble floor. Vines twined thickly, like green serpents, among those columns and trailed their sinuous lengths across the floor. A curious idol, long fallen from a broken pedestal, lay upon the floor and stared up with red, unblinking eyes. The man noted the character of this corroded thing and a strong shudder shook him. He glanced unbelievingly again at the other thing which lay on the marble floor, and shrugged his shoulders.

He entered the shrine. He gazed at the carvings on the bases of the sullen columns, wondering at their unholy and indescribable appearance. Over all the scent of the orchids hung like a heavy fog.

This small, rankly grown, swampy island was once the pinnacle of a great mountain, mused the man, and he wondered what strange people had reared up this fane— and left the monstrous thing lying before the fallen idol. He thought of the fame which his discoveries should bring him—of the acclaim of mighty universities and powerful scientific societies.

He bent above the skeleton on the floor, noting the inhumanly long finger bones, the curious formation of the feet, the deep cavern-like eye sockets, the jutting frontal bone, the general appearance of the great domed skull, which differed so horribly from mankind as he knew it.

What long dead artisan had shaped the thing with such incredible skill? He bent closer, noting the rounded ball-and-socket of the joints, the slight depressions on flat surfaces where muscles had been attached. And he started as the stupendous truth was borne upon him.

This was no work of human art—that skeleton had once been clothed in flesh and had walked and spoken and lived. And this was impossible, his reeling brain told him, for the bones were of solid gold.

The orchids nodded in the shadows of the trees. The shrine lay in purple and black shade. The man brooded above the bones and wondered. How could he know of an elder world sorcery great enough to serve undying hate, by lending that hate a concrete substance, impervious to Time's destructions?

The man laid his hand on the golden skull. A sudden deathly shriek broke the silence. The man in the shrine reeled up, screaming, took a single staggering step and then fell headlong, to lie with writhing limbs on the vine-crossed marble floor.

The orchids showered down on him in a sensuous rain and his blind, clutching hands tore them into exotic fragments as he died. Silence fell and an adder crawled sluggishly from within the golden skull.

lakes covered the ruins of old cities on

201

EPILOG

Then the Cataclysm rocked the world. Atlantis and Lemuria sank, and the Pictish islands were heaved up to form the mountain peaks of a new continent. Sections of the Thurian Continent vanished under the waves, or, sinking, formed great inland lakes and seas. Volcanoes broke forth and terrific earthquakes shook down the shining cities of the empires. Whole nations were blotted out.

The barbarians fared a little better than the civilized races. The inhabitants of the Pictish Islands were destroyed, but a great colony of them, settled among the mountains of Valusia's southern frontier to serve as a buffer against foreign invasion, was untouched. The continental kingdom of the Atlanteans likewise escaped the common ruin, and to it came thousands of their tribesmen in ships from the sinking land. Many Lemurians escaped to the eastern coast of the Thurian Continent, which was comparatively untouched. There they were enslaved by the ancient race which already dwelt there, and their history, for thousands of years, is a history of brutal servitude.

In the western part of the continent, changing conditions created strange forms of plant and animal life. Thick jungles covered the plains, great rivers cut their roads to the sea, wild mountains were heaved up, and lakes covered the ruins of old cities in fertile valleys. To the continental kingdom of the Atlanteans, from sunken areas, swarmed myriads of beasts and savages—ape-men and apes. Forced to battle continually for their lives, they yet managed to retain vestiges of their former state of highly advanced barbarism. Robbed of metals and ores, they became workers in stone like their distant ancestors, and had attained a real artistic level, when their struggling culture came into contact with the powerful Pictish nation. The Picts had also reverted to flint, but had advanced more rapidly in the matter of population and war-science. They had none of the Atlantean's artistic nature; they were a ruder, more practical, more prolific race. They left no pictures painted or carved on ivory, as did their enemies, but they left remarkably efficient flint weapons in plenty.

These stone age kingdoms clashed, and in a series of bloody wars, the outnumbered Atlanteans were hurled back into a state of savagery, and the evolution of the Picts was halted. Five hundred years after the Cataclysm the barbaric kingdoms had vanished. They are now a nation of savages—the Picts—carrying on continual warfare with tribes of savages—the Atlanteans. The Picts had the advantage of numbers and unity, whereas the Atlanteans had fallen into loosely-knit clans. That was the west of that day.

In the distant east, cut off from the rest of the world by the heaving up of gigantic mountains and the forming of a chain of vast lakes, the Lemurians are toiling as slaves of their ancient masters. The far south is still veiled in mystery. Untouched by the Cataclysm, its destiny is still pre-human. Of the civilized races of the Thurian Continent, a remnant of one of the non-Valusian nations dwells among the low mountains of the southeast—the Zhemri. Here and there about the world are scattered clans of apish savages, entirely ignorant of the rise and fall of the great civilizations. But in the far north another people are slowly coming into existence.

At the time of the Cataclysm, a band of savages, whose

development was not much above that of the Neander-thal, fled to the north to escape destruction. They found the snow-countries inhabited only by a species of fero-cious snow-apes—huge shaggy white animals, apparently native to that climate. These they fought and drove beyond the arctic circle, to perish, as the savages thought. The latter, then, adapted themselves to their hardy new environment and throve.

After Pictish–Atlantean wars had destroyed the begin-nings of what might have been a new culture, another, lesser cataclysm further altered the appearance of the original continent, left a great inland sea where the chain of lakes had been, to further separate west from east, and the attendant earthquakes, floods, and volcanoes completed the ruin of the barbarians which their tribal wars had begun.

A thousand years after the lesser cataclysm, the west-ern world is seen to be a wild country of jungles and lakes and torrential rivers. Among the forest-covered hills of the northwest exist wandering bands of ape-men with-out human speech, or the knowledge of fire or the use of implements. They are the descendants of the Atlan-teans, sunk back into the squalling chaos of jungle-bestiality from which ages ago their ancestors so labori-ously crawled. To the southwest dwell scattered the clans of degraded, cave-dwelling savages, whose speech is of the most primitive form, yet who still retain the name of Picts, which has come to mean merely a term designating men—themselves—to distinguish them from the true beasts with which they contend for life and food. It is their only link with their former stage. Neither the squalid Picts nor the apish Atlanteans have any contact with other tribes or peoples.

Far to the east, the Lemurians, levelled almost to a bestial plane themselves by the brutishness of their slav-ery, have risen and destroyed their masters. They are savages stalking among the ruins of a strange civilization. The survivors of that civilization, who have escaped the fury of their slaves, have come westward. They fall upon that mysterious pre-human kingdom of the south and overthrow it, substituting their own culture, modified by contact with the older one. The newer kingdom is called Stygia, and remnants of the older nation seemed to have survived, and even been worshipped, after the race as a whole had been destroyed.

Here and there in the world small groups of savages are showing signs of an upward trend; these are scattered and unclassified. But in the north, the tribes are growing. These people are called Hyborians, or Hybori; their god was Bori—some great chief, whom legend made even more ancient as the king who led them into the north, in the days of the great Cataclysm, which the tribes remember only in distorted folklore.

They had spread over the north, and are pushing southward in leisurely treks. So far they have not come in contact with any other races; their wars have been with one another. Fifteen hundred years in the north country have made them a tall, tawny-haired, gray-eyed race, vigorous and war-like, and already exhibiting a well-defined artistry and poetism of nature. They still live mostly by the hunt, but the southern tribes have been raising cattle for some centuries. There is one exception in their so far complete isolation from other races: a wanderer into the far north returned with the news that the supposedly deserted ice wastes were inhabited by an extensive tribe of ape-like men, descended, he swore, from the beasts driven out of the more habitable land by the ancestors of the Hyborians. He urged that a large war-party be sent beyond the arctic to exterminate these beasts, whom he swore were evolving into true men. He was jeered at; a small band of adventurous young warriors followed him into the north, but none returned.

But tribes of the Hyborians were drifting south, and as the population increased, this movement became extensive. The following age was an epoch of wandering and conquest. Across the history of the world tribes and drifts of tribes moved and shifted in an everchanging panorama.

Look at the world five hundred years later. Tribes of tawny-haired Hyborians have moved southward and westward, conquering and destroying many of the small unclassified clans. Absorbing the blood of conquered races, already the descendants of the older drifts have begun to show modified racial traits, and these mixed races are attacked fiercely by new, purer-blooded drifts, and swept before them as a broom sweeps debris impartially, to become even more mixed and mingled in the tangled debris of races and tag-ends of races.

As yet the conquerors have not come in contact with the older races. To the southeast, the descendants of the Zhemri, given impetus by new blood resulting from admixture with some unclassified tribe, are beginning to seek to revive some faint shadow of their ancient culture. To the west, apish Atlanteans are beginning the long climb upward. They have completed the cycle of existence; they have long forgotten their former existence as men; unaware of any other former state, they are starting the climb unhelped and unhindered by human memories. To the south of them, the Picts remain savages, apparently defying the laws of Nature by neither progressing nor retrogressing. Far to the south dreams the ancient mysterious kingdom of Stygia. On its eastern borders wander clans of nomadic savages, already known as the Sons of Shem.

Next to the Picts, in the broad valley of Zingg, protected by great mountains, a nameless band of primitives, tentatively classified as akin to the Shemites, has evolved an advanced agricultural system and existence.

Another factor has added to the impetus of Hyborian drift. A tribe of that race has discovered the use of stone in building, and the first Hyborian kingdom has come into being—the rude and barbaric kingdom of Hyperborea, which had its beginning in a crude fortress of boulders heaped to repel tribal attack. The people of this tribe soon abandoned their horse-hide tents for stone houses, crudely but mightily built, and thus protected, they grew strong. There are few more dramatic events in history than the rise of the rude, fierce kingdom of Hyperborea, whose people turned abruptly from their nomadic life to rear dwellings of naked stone, surrounded by cyclopean walls—a race scarcely emerged from the polished stone age, who had by a freak of chance, learned the first rude principles of architecture.

The rise of this kingdom drove forth many other tribes, for, defeated in war, or refusing to become tributary to their castle-dwelling kinsmen, many clans set forth on long treks that took them halfway around the world. And already the more northern tribes are beginning to be harried by gigantic blond savages, not much more advanced than ape-men.

The tale of the next thousand years is the tale of the rise of the Hyborians, whose war-like tribes dominate the western world. Rude kingdoms are taking shape. The tawny-haired invaders have encountered the Picts, driving them into the barren lands of the west. To the northwest, the descendants of the Atlanteans, climbing unaided from apedom into primitive savagery, have not yet met the conquerors. Far to the east, the Lemurians are evolving a strange semi-civilization of their own. To the south, the Hyborians have founded the kingdom of Koth, on the borders of those pastoral countries known as the lands of Shem, and the savages of those lands, partly through contact with the Hyborians, partly through contact with the Stygians who have ravaged them for centuries, are emerging from barbarism. The blond savages of the far north have grown in power and numbers so that the northern Hyborian tribes move southward, driving their kindred clans before them. The ancient kingdom of Hyperborea is overthrown by one of those northern tribes, which, however, retains the old name. Southeast of Hyperborea, a kingdom of the Zhemri has come into being, under the name of Zamora. To the southwest, a tribe of Picts has invaded the fertile valley of Zingg, conquered the agricultural people there, and settled among them. This mixed race was in turn conquered later by a roving tribe of Hybori, and from these mingled elements came the kingdom of Zingara.

Five hundred years later, the kingdoms of the world are clearly defined. The kingdoms of the Hyborians—Aquilonia, Nemedia, Brythunia, Hyperborea, Koth, Ophir, Argos, Corinthia, and one known as the Border Kingdom—dominate the western world. Zamora lies to the east, and Zingara to the southwest of these kingdoms—peoples alike in darkness of complexion and exotic habits, but otherwise unrelated. Far to the south sleeps Stygia, untouched by foreign invasion, but the people of Shem have exchanged the Stygian yoke for the less galling one of Koth. The dusky masters have been driven south of the great river Styx, Nilus, or Nile, which, flowing north from the shadowy hinterlands turns almost at right angles and flows almost due west through the pastoral meadowlands of Shem, to empty into the great sea. North of Acquilonia, the westernmost Hyborian kingdom, are the Cimmerians, ferocious savages, untamed by the invaders, but advancing rapidly because of contact with them; they are the descendants of the Atlanteans, now progressing more steadily than their old enemies, the Picts, who dwell in the wilderness west of Aquilonia.

—The Hyborian Age

ANNOUNCING:
THE ARCANA

A GROUNDBREAKING NEW SERIES FROM THE BESTSELLING AUTHOR OF *LION OF IRELAND!*

They are **The Arcana.** Collectively, they are the ultimate symbols of cosmic power. Millennia ago they were the treasures of the gods of creation, honored and cherished in four great cities since swept away by the rivers of time. The Spear of Light came from Gorias. The city of Falias contained The Stone of Destiny. From Murias came The Cup of Blood. The Sword of Flame was enshrined within Findias.

Properly used by an adept, these four together have the power to create worlds—or to destroy them. The three volumes of The Arcana by Morgan Llywelyn and Michael Scott tell of the desperate quest to rediscover the ancient tools of creation and restore a world that lives only in memory. A world everyone longs to return to, in their most secret dreams. The lost world at the outermost limit of human desire.

Book One tells the story of Silverhand, he who was foretold, he who is destined to save the world from Chaos and begin the long climb back to the world that lives within us all.

To Read About Great Characters Having Incredible Adventures You Should Try 🖝 🖝 🖝

BAEN

IF YOU LIKE...YOU SHOULD TRY...

Norse Mythology... *The Mask of Loki* by
Roger Zelazny & Thomas T. Thomas

The Iron Thane by Jason Henderson

Sleipnir by Linda Evans

Puns... *Mall Purchase Night* by Rick Cook

The Case of the Toxic Spell Dump
by Harry Turtledove

Quests... *Pigs Don't Fly* and *The Unlikely Ones*
by Mary Brown

The Deed of Paksenarrion by Elizabeth Moon

Through the Ice by Piers Anthony & Robert Kornwise

Vampires... *Tomorrow Sucks*
by Greg Cox & T.K.F. Weisskopf

Paksenarrion, a simple sheepfarmer's daughter, yearns for a life of adventure and glory, such as the heroes in songs and story. At age seventeen she runs away from home to join a mercenary company, and begins her epic life . . .

ELIZABETH MOON

THE DEED OF PAKSENARRION

"This is the first work of high heroic fantasy I've seen, that has taken the work of Tolkien, assimilated it totally and deeply and absolutely, and produced something altogether new and yet incontestably based on the master. . . . This is the real thing. Worldbuilding in the grand tradition, background thought out to the last detail, by someone who knows absolutely whereof she speaks. . . . Her military knowledge is impressive, her picture of life in a mercenary company most convincing."—**Judith Tarr**

About the author: Elizabeth Moon joined the U.S. Marine Corps in 1968 and completed both Officers Candidate School and Basic School, reaching the rank of 1st Lieutenant during active duty. Her background in military training and discipline imbue The Deed of Paksenarrion *with a gritty realism that is all too rare in most current fantasy.*

"I thoroughly enjoyed *Deed of Paksenarrion*. A most engrossing highly readable work."
—**Anne McCaffrey**

"For once the promises are borne out. *Sheep-farmer's Daughter* is an advance in realism. . . . I can only say that I eagerly await whatever Elizabeth Moon chooses to write next."
—Taras Wolansky, *Lan's Lantern*

*   *   *   *   *

Volume One: Sheepfarmer's Daughter—Paks is trained as a mercenary, blooded, and introduced to the life of a soldier . . . and to the followers of Gird, the soldier's god.

Volume Two: Divided Allegiance—Paks leaves the Duke's company to follow the path of Gird alone—and on her lonely quests encounters the other sentient races of her world.

Volume Three: Oath of Gold—Paks the warrior must learn to live with Paks the human. She undertakes a holy quest for a lost elven prince that brings the gods' wrath down on her and tests her very limits.

*   *   *   *   *

These books are available at your local bookstore, or you can fill out the coupon and return it to Baen Books, at the address below.

SHEEPFARMER'S DAUGHTER • 65416-0 • 506 pp • $5.99   ____
DIVIDED ALLEGIANCE • 69786-2 • 528 pp • $5.99   ____
OATH OF GOLD • 69798-6 • 528 pp • $3.95   ____
or get all three volumes in one special trade paperback edition,
THE DEED OF PAKSENARRION • 72104-4 • 1,040 pp • $15.00 ____

Please send the cover price to: Baen Books, Dept. BA, P.O. Box 1403, Riverdale, NY 10471.
Name_____
Address_____
City_____ State_____ Zip_____

GRAND ADVENTURE

IN GAME-BASED UNIVERSES

With these exciting novels set
in bestselling game universes,
Baen brings you synchronicity at its
best. We believe that familiarity with
either the novel or the game will
intensify enjoyment of the other.
All novels are the only authorized
fiction based on these games and
are published by permission.

THE BARD'S TALE™

Join the Dark Elf Naitachal and his apprentices in bardic
magic as they explore the mysteries of the world of
The Bard's Tale.

Castle of Deception   0-671-72125-9 ◆ $5.99 ☐
Mercedes Lackey & Josepha Sherman

Fortress of Frost and Fire   0-671-72162-3 ◆ $5.99 ☐
Mercedes Lackey & Ru Emerson

Prison of Souls   0-671-72193-3 ◆ $5.99 ☐
Mercedes Lackey & Mark Shepherd

The Chaos Gate   0-671-87597-3 ◆ $5.99 ☐
Josepha Sherman

(continued)

WING COMMANDER™

The computer game which supplies the background world for these novels is a current all-time bestseller. Fly with the best the Confederation of Earth has to offer against the ferocious catlike alien Kilrathi!

Freedom Flight   0-671-72145-3 ◆ $4.99 ☐
Mercedes Lackey & Ellen Guon

End Run   0-671-72200-X ◆ $4.99 ☐
Christopher Stasheff & William R. Forstchen

Fleet Action   0-671-72211-5 ◆ $4.99 ☐
William R. Forstchen

Heart of the Tiger   0-671-87653-8 ◆ $5.99 ☐
William R. Forstchen & Andrew Keith

STARFIRE™

See this strategy game come to explosive life in these grand space adventures!

Insurrection   0-671-72024-4 ◆ $5.99 ☐
David Weber & Steve White

Crusade   0-671-72111-9 ◆ $4.99 ☐
David Weber & Steve White

- -

MERCEDES LACKEY

The Hottest Fantasy Writer Today!

URBAN FANTASY

Knight of Ghosts and Shadows with Ellen Guon
Elves in L.A.? It would explain a lot, wouldn't it? Eric
Banyon really needed a good cause to get his life in
gear—now he's got one. With an elven prince he must
raise an army to fight against the evil elf lord who seeks
to conquer all of California.

Summoned to Tourney with Ellen Guon
Elves in San Francisco? Where else would an elf go
when L.A. got too hot? All is well there with our elf-lord,
his human companion and the mage who brought them
all together—until it turns out that San Francisco is
doomed to fall off the face of the continent.

Born to Run with Larry Dixon
There are elves out there. And more are coming. But
even elves need money to survive in the "real" world.
The good elves in South Carolina, intrigued by the thrills
of stock car racing, are manufacturing new, light-weight
engines (with, incidentally, very little "cold" iron); the bad
elves run a kiddie-porn and snuff-film ring, with occa-
sional forays into drugs. *Children in Peril—Elves to the
Rescue.* (Book I of the SERRAted Edge series.)

Wheels of Fire with Mark Shepherd
Book II of the SERRAted Edge series.

When the Bough Breaks with Holly Lisle
Book III of the SERRAted Edge series.

HIGH FANTASY

Bardic Voices: The Lark & The Wren
Rune could be one of the greatest bards of her world, but the daughter of a tavern wench can't get much in the way of formal training. So one night she goes up to play for the Ghost of Skull Hill. She'll either fiddle till dawn to prove her skill as a bard—or die trying....

The Robin and the Kestrel: Bardic Voices II
After the affairs recounted in *The Lark and The Wren*, Robin, a gypsy lass and bard, and Kestrel, semi-fugitive heir to a throne he does not want, have married their fortunes together and travel the open road, seeking their happiness where they may find it. This is their story. It is also the story of the Ghost of Skull Hill. Together, the Robin, the Kestrel, and the Ghost will foil a plot to drive all music forever from the land....

Bardic Choices: A Cast of Corbies with Josepha Sherman

If I Pay Thee Not in Gold with Piers Anthony
A new hardcover quest fantasy, co-written by the creator of the "Xanth" series. A marvelous adult fantasy that examines the war between the sexes and the ethics of desire! Watch out for bad puns!

BARD'S TALE

Based on the bestselling computer game, *The Bard's Tale.*®

Castle of Deception with Josepha Sherman

Fortress of Frost and Fire with Ru Emerson

Prison of Souls with Mark Shepherd

Also by Mercedes Lackey:

Reap the Whirlwind with C.J. Cherryh
Part of the Sword of Knowledge series.

The Ship Who Searched with Anne McCaffrey
The Ship Who Sang is not alone!

Wing Commander: Freedom Flight with Ellen Guon
Based on the bestselling computer game, *Wing Commander.*℠

Join the Mercedes Lackey national fan club! For information send an SASE (business-size) to Queen's Own, P.O. Box 43143, Upper Montclair, NJ 07043.